Advanced International Acclaim for *White Ghost in China*

"A fascinating story set in China with many insights into the country, written by an author with intimate knowledge of the people and customs. Good reading." - *Mike Saxon, author of An American's Guide to Doing Business in China*

"For someone who only reads non-fiction, this fictional debut caught my attention and held it throughout the story. It was imaginative, mystical and magical - I felt like I was there, and I learned a few things about China-when can we expect the sequel?" - *Paul Niemann, syndicated newspaper columnist of "Red, White and True Mysteries," USA*

"Understanding how business dealings work in China I found this as powerful writing and it kept me on the edge of the seat." - *Willy Haugland, Molda, Norway*

"I was absolutely captivated from the first sentence on -a great story. Cheers!" - *Christine Keen, Brisbane, Australia*

"Wow! What a great read-taut, vibrant, richly textured and inspired me as a reader." - *Dilceia Arcino, Puerto Allegra, Brazil*

WHITE GHOST
In China

A NOVEL BY

Gary Kellmann & Michael Kuhn

A Lost American in China

彷徨 *Fear* 愛情 *Love* 归宿 *Destiny*

White Ghost Global, LLC

16769 Babler View Drive

Wildwood, MO 63011

First edition published in 2008

The Library of Congress has catalogued the paperback edition as follows:

Kellmann, Gary and Kuhn, Michael.
White Ghost in China a novel/Gary Kellmann, Michael Kuhn—1st ed.
fiction—China—inspirational journey. 2. Kellmann—Kuhn—destiny
fear—love—Shenzhen—China—white ghost 3. mother—woman—mystical
4. based on true events—mafia—love story—Wal-Mart—ghost
5. inspiration—fiction

ISBN-13: 978-0-9799522-9-6
ISBN-10:   Q-9799522-9-8
LCCN: # 2007936885

The first edition of White Ghost in China is printed in U.S.A.

Book cover and White Ghost in China logo designed by Robert Leuschke.

*This is dedicated to
those who have adopted children from China,
and have brought back so much joy and
love to our country*

Prologue

Destiny, dream, delusion…call it by whatever you believe in. Not only do I believe in destiny but I fear it like some people fear spiders or heights or failure. Yeah, me, Ben Stillwater from a small farming town, Owensville, Missouri, who made my first small fortune from the loft of a neighbor's barn where I kept inventory imported from China, and then sold the Chinese flashing toys and bracelets to local businesses. Bored with the ins and outs of other people's stuff, I started puttering, making things, inventing.

After suddenly getting lucky on an invention no bigger than a bellybutton, the Belly Light, the one that kick-started my gold rush fever as it did with so many others who spotted China as the next big "thing," I flew west to make my fortune in the East—in Shenzhen, China, the electronic toy capital of the world. This was where an idealistic American could strike it rich.

In my wallet, I kept a tiny bit of wisdom from my childhood—a fortune cookie prophecy. It read "Your destiny lies beyond your fear." I hoped to find my destiny in China.

But I didn't expect to deal with the mafia, up close and bloodily personal. I didn't expect to fall in love. And I didn't expect the ghost.

One

First of all, there was the comfort of the Grey Wolf, a thank-God-for-this-place restaurant in Shenzhen. Not only was the food good, but it was a place that helped me transition from back home to this noisy banging country of contradictions. I had been in China for only a few weeks when I found it tucked among some twenty-story buildings.

"Nee-how," I said, greeting the server who handed me a menu. He smiled, bowed slightly. I smiled and opened the menu. Good, I had mastered "hello." Now, what the hell did the menu say?

Trish and Al would be joining me any minute for dinner. They could translate. They would like this place; I found it myself and was eager for them to approve of my good taste.

I picked up the chopsticks at my place setting and drew them from their paper wrapper, rubbed them together, and slotted the utensils between my thumb and index finger. As happened, though less often since my arrival, I was swept up in old memories of home, like when I was eight or nine and Dad would bring home boxes of sweet-and-sour pork and cashew chicken on Monday nights. We loved opening the white paper cartons, always surprised at the contents and the challenge of getting through the meal with chopsticks. Dad insisted we try using them. Mom was always patient and had forks in her apron pocket, just in case.

Now a foreigner in Shenzhen, trying to make it my new home, I appreciated the light disposable wood sticks for what they were. Less abrupt than steel forks and knives. Kinder. Efficient. Graceful, really.

*****

Back home, I wouldn't answer my cell at the table. It was a courtesy thing. But here, phones rang in a constant chorus and conversations were always in progress, at the dining table, in the store, on the street, or while driving a scooter one-handed with a toddler balanced on the crotch of the seat in front of the driver. So before entering the restaurant, I had returned a call to some neighbors at home whose message asked me how things were going. I didn't want to talk with them, actually, and was hoping now to get their message machine. If I connected with Anne or Joe whose barn I had used in the old days (what? only several months ago?), I knew there would be a catch in my voice and Anne would hear it and insist on my return to the States. She was always far more vocal than my own mom about my current adventure. Just be careful; just be sure everyone is nice to you, Anne would always say. Like a chant. Like a mantra.

There was no answer. I left a brief message and went into the Grey Wolf to be shown to my favorite table.

*****

I stopped fiddling with the chopsticks and turned to admire the food being served at the table just next to me. I was starving. I imagined moving my chair over there and digging into the food with the couple that was about to enjoy plates heaped with noodles and vegetables and bowls of something fragrant, I didn't care. What would they think?

"Ben!"

"Hi, Ben!"

It was Al and Trish, just in time, waving at me and hurrying toward my table, each lugging briefcases that looked to be jampacked with papers. I stood to greet them, shaking hands with Al, holding a chair for Trish, waiting for her to sit while she first peered around the restaurant.

"It looks like you made a good choice, Ben."

"Thanks, I hope you enjoy the food as much as the atmosphere," I said.

The Grey Wolf was a Shenzhen anomaly: the exterior resembled a mud hut but inside, it was cozy in tones of brown and grey, and dramatic with thatched pendant lights, aged wood tables, kabuki masks and animal skulls hung intermittently on the walls. At the entrance, a large post-World War II poster proclaimed the area off-limits to "militaristic-minded Japanese." Gauzy sheets painted with Chinese symbols softened the rustic ceiling and a small balcony protruded over the bar, apparently just for looks. Hidden speakers poured ambient music into the room, and I was glad to have escaped from the American '80s music piped into most Shenzhen restaurants.

"How's business?" I asked them as the waiter appeared and handed them menus. Thank God, I thought. Let's order and eat. I wasn't really interested in business, not yet.

"Not so good. We just had a meeting at the factory," Al said without looking at his menu. He leaned toward me. "Retooling costs have doubled the wholesale price for the action figures we are producing. I wish I worked in solar panels like you, Ben. 'Green' business means lots of green in your pocket, right? This toy business is hard. I mean, it is difficult, right?" Al smiled. I knew him well enough to understand his smile was a cover; I knew the business well enough that he was hurting.

"Trust me, the solar business is not all it's cracked up to be," I said. "But with this idea we've come up with, a new line of solar-powered toy trains, well, I think we may just have a winner here."

"Al mentioned this idea to me. So how do solar-powered toys work inside?" Trish asked. "Won't they need sunlight?"

"And that," I replied, "is a very good question. But these aren't toy trains for indoor use. They're different. Kids will play with them outside, in the sandbox, on a backyard patio, even on the lawn. The

6

point is to get kids out of the house and into fresh air. No wires, no batteries."

Trish nodded and smiled. "Interesting," she said. "That is a very unique concept."

"Well that's what Al and I are trying to do, create an interesting toy."

Though Al and Trish had taken English names as so many Chinese did, they weren't fluent in American slang. I was glad the Chinese had taken English monikers since I'd given up on pronouncing the names. And, it was good for business, Al had told me. Newborns were given English names, and older citizens eventually adopted one.

"Let's be upbeat. After all, Ben, we talked you into coming. Here's to making successful business and much much money. Let's eat and celebrate."

I nodded, playing with my chopsticks.

Halfway through a sumptuous meal, Al looked at his watch, then leaned toward me. "I have a meeting in twenty minutes. Would you see that Trish gets home? And I will talk to you later—you have my new cell number, right?"

"Oh, sure." I looked across the table at Trish. She nodded and smiled and kept eating.

"I'll be sure she gets home."

Al folded his napkin next to his dish, stood, picked up his briefcase, nodded to each of us, turned and walked quickly toward the door, stopping to say something to our server and press something into his hand. Then he was gone.

Trish and I looked at our plates and kept eating. My chopstick abilities or rather lack thereof had her giggling with delight.

"Want a fork?" Trish asked.

"No. Thanks." I tried desperately to capture some noodles that were wriggling between the chopsticks and back into the bowl.

Alone, I might have used my fingers, but the social embarrassment of resorting to caveman food-handling tactics kept me at it. I really wanted to fit in, at least at this table.

"This coriander lamb is excellent. I'd never tried lamb until I found this place. Sure we're not eating dog?" I asked.

"You never know, Ben. The Chinese will eat anything on four legs. Except the table," she said.

I stopped, chopsticks mid-air, meat falling back to the dish.

"I'm kidding," she said. "Sure you don't want a fork?"

"Hey, I'm good at this. See?" But the next piece of lamb fell into my lap. "Dammit." For some reason, I found myself thinking of one of those choose-your-own-adventure books I had read as a kid where every couple of pages, you had two or three choices, so the plot ran in any one of several possible directions. You could live or die, the choice was yours. Choose your own adventure, Ben. OK, here it was—eating with a business associate. I had to deflect attention from me and my chopsticks.

"Ever go ghost hunting?" I asked Trish.

"Changing the subject?" she said.

I liked Trish. She was gorgeous and all business. I used the word "gorgeous" a lot, but she was. Trish wasted little conversation on small

8

talk, she dressed to impress in designer suits (she apparently loved Chanel). She was also very well-organized, her briefcase a model of uncluttered, precise papers.

Al dressed well, but he was her not-so-glamorous counterpart with his balding pate, and sagging posture. However, they tag-teamed brilliantly. They were the yin and yang of the manufacturing company I was working with.

"I do OK with chopsticks; I just need a little more practice. So," I continued, looking at her across the table, "Do the Chinese believe in ghosts?"

"Of course. We are very superstitious. If you sneeze, it means someone is thinking of you. As for numbers, some are very good luck, some are very bad, like the number four. Four is bad. And yes, of course we have ghosts here."

"How about ghost hunting?"

"Hunting?"

"Ghost hunting. Looking for them on purpose. You know, going to haunted houses and stuff. Spirits. Visiting graveyards. Stuff like that."

She shook her head. Nope, it wasn't translating.

Holding the sticks with the tips of my index fingers and thumbs, I crossed and uncrossed the chopsticks, and I told her I was "dowsing" for ghosts. I stood, and held out my hands, and zombie-walked around the table. "Ghosts, looking for ghosts, anyone seen any ghosts around here?" The servers at their stations watched me from under their bleach-dyed bangs.

Trish rolled her eyes and giggled, and I pointed the chopsticks at my chest.

"Oh man! I'm the ghost! It's me!" Indeed I was the White Ghost; it was not so much a nickname as a tag because of my white skin. I was one of few in Shenzhen's manufacturing district.

Trish waved her hand, fluttering it as if to say, I am embarrassed, please sit.

True, I would never have done such a thing in a restaurant back home in Missouri. I sat. There are things you do in a foreign country that you might not consider doing back home.

"What was that word you said?" she asked.

"Which word?"

"Drowsy. Drowsing."

"Oh. Dowsing. It's a technique for finding water, or ghosts. Or at least that's what I've heard."

"I don't understand."

"I'm not exactly clear on it, either. I don't think I even believe it. But when I was a kid, my folks took me to a haunted mansion in St. Louis, two hours from the small town where I grew up. The Lemp Mansion is famous, sort of. We had dinner there, and afterward, a psychic—"

"A what?"

"A psychic, a fortune-teller, she gets us all in a group and tells us the mansion was haunted, that ghosts were everywhere in the mansion. The family that had lived there a century ago had a bunch of money. And they were crazy. Anyway, the psychic had these metal rods, bent into L-shapes, and she told us to hold them out in front of us. If the rods crossed, it meant that we were near spiritual energy. Near a ghost."

"Did you find one, a ghost I mean?"

"No. I was pretty creeped out, though. Then she led us to the attic, and I remember hearing a baby cry. But there was no baby in the group. I didn't ask if anyone else heard it. I was embarrassed, I guess, but it made my hair stand up."

Trish leaned across the table, listening.

"The psychic said the family had a son, a kid who was mentally challenged or deformed, or both, and that he lived in the attic with his nurse. The poor kid would peer out the mansard windows, and see other kids down below, leading normal turn-of-the-century kid lives. And they would look up and see his disfigured face. Apparently, they called him The Monkey Boy."

"Was it a baby cry you heard, Ben? Do you think you heard a ghost?"

"Maybe." I paused, for drama and to zone in on the memory. "I do know that in the circle, the psychic turned to me and said the boy's spirit was drawn to me. And then…"

"Yes?"

"And then I felt a tiny hand reaching into my pockets and I froze. Solid. Then the hand was gone."

Trish sat back in her chair, still listening, her mouth a small "o."

"When we were about to leave, I asked the psychic about the Monkey Boy and his nurse. I asked her if the boy stayed close to his nurse. She said of course he did, and that he had this habit of holding on to her pockets as she walked about the house, a childish gesture, right? Kind of like holding onto Mom's apron strings, I guess."

"And you think he was holding on to you?"

"Probably my mind was playing tricks on me, that's what I really think." I didn't tell her that I had felt that ghostly presence at my side, tugging my pocket the whole time we were in the attic until we descended again to the first floor. I had forgotten all about that event, years ago and thousands of miles away.

"You are a receptor," she said. "A ghost whisperer."

"No, no. Not me," I said and laughed. "So, had enough? Ready to head home?"

She shook her head yes, pushed her plate away, dabbed at her lips with her napkin and rose from her seat.

I signaled the waiter who waved me away, smiling.

"It's OK, Ben. Al already paid," Trish said

"But..."

"No, it's all taken care of," she said, hiking her briefcase to her shoulder. "Ready?" And without waiting for my response, she walked toward the lobby.

"Xie xie," I said smiling as I passed the waiter on my way out. My mouth released the sounds easily, the shi-shi sound of "thank you." But I was remembering a dream I had upon my arrival in China. That gorgeous tattooed ghost. Creepy though and surely based on indigestion. It was nothing. Of course not and she had not visited again. I was not a ghost whisperer.

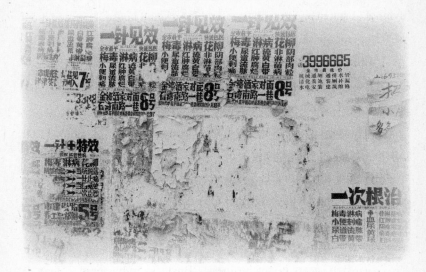

Two

*W*e took our time walking to her apartment, and I was looking around, still curious about this new country that I was calling home, still seeing it even after several months, through a newcomer's eyes. As we passed an alley, I saw a flash of color out of the corner of my eye. Turning, I saw red banners emblazoned with black calligraphy lining the shadowy corridor. I stopped and watched them sway in the evening breeze.

"Trish, what are the banners for?"

"Autumn Moon Festival. Important holiday for Chinese, mid-autumn festival." She said. "Families get together, eat moon cakes and sing moon poems. Also a night for lovers," she added with a smile.

I looked up at one of the banners. It bore a glyph, a lone Chinese symbol. I stared and thought it resembled a small house. I pointed it out to Trish, and she said it meant "think."

"Think of what, exactly?" I asked.

"Think of what is in your heart, Ben."

I wasn't exactly sure where she was coming from. My heart?

"My heart had better be about this business venture," I laughed. "Or I won't be staying here long."

She looked confused, and I remembered I should speak in short sentences to make it easier for her to understand.

"My heart," I said. "My heart is in my business. Or I will have to leave here."

"No, Ben, heart is not business. Business is business. Heart is family. Friends."

"And ghosts," I said. "You are doing business with a ghost. Me!"

"I don't understand," she stopped and looked at me.

"The kids call me gui-lao," I explained. "Al said it means 'white ghost.'" I pronounced the word gway-low, elongating the first syllable.

Seeing me smile, she giggled and covered her mouth.

I produced the chopsticks from my pocket. I was going to fiddle with them later, fashion something with them. Now I pointed them straight ahead and said, "We're going to dowse the alley." I started creeping down the concrete passageway, Trish following behind me.

"Where are the ghosts?" I was deep into the charade now. "Ghosts, come out, come out, wherever you are! Nee-how, ghosts," I called, "Hello?"

Trish laughed and shoved me.

We turned a corner, laughing and dowsing, when suddenly out of nowhere we were surrounded by a group of men. I dropped the chopsticks and put my arm around Trish, holding her to my side.

Their body language stabbed at the air around us. Anger prickled from their glares and steely mouths, and I had no idea why, didn't care why, and at the moment was trying to figure out how to save us from being robbed or beaten. I remembered witnessing the aftermath of a tragic mugging a month ago. Both assailant and victim ended up dead. I had heard rumors of gangs entering buses and beating and robbing all the unlucky passengers. A machete, I had been told, was often used by motorcycle muggers; drive-bys involved the dismembering of some poor woman's arm, in order to steal her purse. There were stories and rumors of mafia clans breaking into a person's house and holding them ransom until a debt was paid.

I clutched my backpack in one hand, the other still encircling Trish. "What's going on?"

"Shssssh," she whispered. "Al! Call Al!" Then she jerked her arm away and stood straight up, defying the group to make a move.

I knelt down as if tying my shoe. In the process, I slid my hand into my pants pocket and pressed the redial on my cell. Al answered and I dropped my voice to a forceful whisper.

"Al, we need help! Some guys have us in the alleyway close to your apartment. Come now!" I stood, and grabbed the strap of my backpack. Since it was loaded with my laptop and books, I figured it for a decent weapon. Trish was speaking to them in Mandarin, and I tried to follow the volley of alien words. I had no idea who was saying what—or who was winning the war of words.

"What do I do?" I looked at Trish.

She glared at me, and I was trying to figure out what was going on and if I should do something. Men are supposed to be the protectors, right?

I decided to make a move. I began cursing and swinging my laptop rucksack, hoping to make brutal contact with someone. The shortest goon, no more than five feet tall, wore an outfit of white: white pants, white t-shirt, even matching white sneakers. On his head, two ball caps were turned in opposite directions, a black L.A. Raiders cap somehow fastened on top of a white Pittsburgh Pirates ballcap. He was dressed like the bastard offspring of an L.A. gangbanger and Napoleon Bonaparte. Later, I would learn he admired the famous Frenchman, and had even adopted his name.

He flashed a sadistic grin, showing a grill of gold teeth. Before he made good his intent, I read in his eyes, "I really want to hurt you." Producing an expandable whiprod, he stepped forward, swung it once, and made perfect contact with my ribs causing an excruciating shot of pain that left me doubled over in agony, wondering what was broken and would I ever straighten up again.

Trish jumped in front of the midget gangster to shield me, and he stepped back. I sat on the ground, holding my midsection and trying to breathe, sucking in the available oxygen, holding in tears. Trish began shouting at the crew, like a football center protecting a fallen quarterback.

Besides the incapacitating pain, I was embarrassed to have been knocked down so easily by so slight a man. Frightened of potential weapon escalation, I stayed down. I didn't want to see knives or guns.

In the midst of the commotion, I felt a pair of hands on my back, ever so lightly. I jerked around, losing my breath again in doing so, to see a thick mane of hair framing a beautiful, pale face, the face of the full moon as its light falls gentle and calm.

"Come," she insisted, and with surprising strength, this slender apparition pulled me to my feet. "You're OK," she said as if this were an everyday occurrence. She smiled, then disappeared into the night.

Three

*B*efore the attack in the alley, before I was to fall in love with a mysterious girl, before I started writing long letters home like a kid at camp, and before I came to grips with the intricacies of doing business in Shenzhen, I was just a foreigner in a foreign land.

I would wake up coughing and hacking as I slowly adjusted to the city's pollution. I gave up the idea of wearing a mask; I already stood out, towering over those around me.

I was ready to conquer the language with computer software and a translation book. The very idea earned my personal derision. I was naïve to think such tools would be all I needed, though they did help.

I was here to unlock my destiny; China was my path. Heroic words, I suppose, even a little nineteenth century, but that was my intent. That, and making lots of money. I mean, a lot.

Shenzhen, formerly a city of eleven-thousand residents, had become a manufacturing powerhouse of millions of people in only a few years' time. I wound up in Bao'an, a small manufacturing district within Shenzhen, a forty-minute ferry ride and half-hour taxi trip north of the westernized world of Hong Kong. But Hong Kong might as well have been thousands of miles away from what was about to become my new home.

Welcome to southeastern China, white man.

*****

Upon my arrival, a coastal fog smeared the taxi's windshield as we rocketed away from the airport and into the city but the driver was oblivious and drummed on his car door to the beat of techno pop blaring from his radio. We rolled through streets walled in by concrete block buildings and factories and crammed with bikes, mopeds, dogs, and throngs of people. It was impossible to tell if they were headed home or to work. It was 8 a.m.

The city air was infused with sulfur. I was going to choke and die, right here in the taxi. I felt like Superman stuck in a kryptonite cell. Thoughts of home came unbidden, images of Missouri summers with a July sun and August oven that turned green grass to brown straw and sidewalks white-hot.

Stop it, I told myself, coughing into my sleeve. Sit up. Deal. I shook my head, forced myself to stare out the window. And still the cab driver hummed and tap tap tapped, now on his dashboard. He had obviously developed some sort of evolutionary secondary breathing apparatus that allowed him to function. Maybe he had gills or a third lung hidden beneath his Mao jacket. Perhaps they all had. Perhaps I would evolve, too.

The decrepit motel where I imagined Al and Trish had put me up turned out to be a new, four-star hotel. Its name, "The Bossman" was lit vertically along one side. My relief was so apparent that the cab driver turned and asked, "You are so happy to be here, yes?"

I should have trusted the intrepid Al and Trish to take care of me. After all, I'd been doing business with them stateside for several years, but still I had imagined being housed like a migrant, humbly, throwing myself on some sort of pallet at day's end, grateful for a clean cup of tea. Maybe I could stop being fearful, at least a little.

In fact, there was plenty of new local construction; I had to give Shenzhen credit for its forward motion. I would soon find that all the "modern" conveniences like plumbing and electricity and cleanliness were available, albeit at various levels of quality, and that I had absolutely no reason to worry about any imagined medieval conditions. Jeez, I could be a fearful shit sometimes.

I managed paying, and I think tipping, the taxi driver, then walked into the hotel lobby where my unshaven, untucked, very lanky and white-skinned appearance instantly became the center of attention. I was the focus of several dozen expressionless stares. This, then, was the beginning of "White Ghost," a tag I was to carry for many, many months. The concierge was the first to call me "gui-lao," or ghost-man, but eventually I wore the more stylish moniker: White Ghost.

And this white ghost had needed a little persuasion from his Chinese business partner and friend, Al.

"I'm a little afraid to just hop across the Pacific and start living in a foreign country," I told him.

"To fulfill destiny, you must face your fear," Al had told me months ago. Oh baby, I'm on a mission to do that, I thought.

The desk clerk handed me my room key, and two girls attended to my paltry baggage.

So, this was the place. I was shaking. I only hoped it wasn't noticeable.

*****

The next several days were a blur. It was a crash course in Intro to China.

The people were not at all used to Americans. Their stereotypes of us were as unfounded and overblown as ours were of their culture. Didn't all Americans drive enormous SUVs? No. Didn't all Chinese eat dogs for dinner? No. Didn't all Americans live in mansions? No. Didn't all Chinese want to raise only sons? No.

Both countries were huge consumers. Yes. Both had their arms wrapped figuratively and financially around the world. Yes. Which country would lead was a question best left unanswered.

At breakfast that first morning, I experienced their presumption of how Americans ate. I ordered eggs and received five plates of poorly scrambled stuff—brown, oily, and inedible. Apparently no one spoke English and I was the first and only Westerner in the place. At least that's what I somehow came to understand from one of the staff, who I named George. The hotel's restaurant actually catered to the local market of Chinese factory workers and their out-of-town guests, not to out-of-country guests.

My appearance was the cause of daily intrigue. At every meal, three or four different girls surrounded me, ready to serve. I couldn't finish a plate of food before the last bite was whisked away. Everyone wanted to serve; everyone wanted to be in on the action I might stir up.

I wanted cold drinks; they were served warm. Ice was not to be found. I may as well have requested gold coins in my diet cola. Some translation, I mused, must be absent. No, the Chinese didn't use ice in their drinks I soon discovered. I was forced into the lukewarm custom. So far, there was no choice. But surely refrigerators had freezers, and somewhere there were ice cubes? I would have one, quickly scribbling that on my list of goals.

Eggs, however, became my obsession. The hotel cook continued to misunderstand my request for scrambled. Boiled, OK; sunny side up, OK; or, poached, OK, but never properly scrambled. The eggs were burned, runny, and just plain revolting.

And then one day the chef got it right. I was presented one morning with a fluffy mound of golden eggs, buttery and rich. It was cause for celebration. The waitress, the cook, and I smiled at one another and I stood to shake their hands. There was gastronomic hope after all, the bliss of one thing being just right.

Dinner would continue to be another story. Fish head soup; plucked duck and full round chickens served in toto, with eyeballs glazed with the mask of death; and turtle with bizarre vegetables. These were regular buffet entrees. As I came to know the staff, I suggested, I complained, yes, I begged for some Western dishes. I showed the cook (when he asked, and he did) different websites with recipes for hamburgers, fried chicken, and steak. Simple stuff.

"No problem," the manager would say, and still, nothing ever changed. "No problem," I found, was a Chinese way of saying, "Not likely." I learned. I acquiesced. I grew thinner.

George was the hotel's assistant manager. He loved the American name I gave him on the first day. He repeated whenever possible, referring to himself in the third person so he could use it: "George thinks you'll like this" and "George had an enjoyable evening" and so on.

He stood in front of me one morning, beaming and pointing at his name tag, a bright, gold rectangle above his left pocket. It read "George." This attracted the staff's attention, and soon I was bombarded with requests for American names. I now could ask favors of Christina, Brian, Nora, Adam, and my precious cook, Festus.

*****

Beyond the hotel's walls, despite the race to build new businesses and dwellings, there remained the chipped grey apartment buildings and dormitories. I had no idea who inhabited these places until I learned much later that it was where factory workers lived. So did the hotel's four-hundred employees. I had somehow imagined the hotel staff had luxurious rooms, similar to mine, only stuck in the basement or lower floor, much like crew members on a cruise ship. Anyway, loathe to be called out for my foreign looks or beat up and left for dead by youngsters who knew the local game, I stuck close to the hotel grounds, afraid for my safety. I worked constantly from my room, rarely leaving my laptop or phone, both my connections to the outside world of Shenzhen and beyond.

Shenzhen was the epicenter of electronic toys in China. This was where U.S. businesses made their millions. A high-tech neighborhood surrounded by the ghetto.

In hindsight, I wasn't particularly wrong in my suppositions. There were tough neighborhoods out there, a mere degree of separation from where I was staying. I realized how the place had taken away some of my swagger.

My hotel friends helped acquaint me with the neighborhoods. I felt safe with them and grateful for their company. I eventually mapped out a two-mile radius, and began walking my "territory" at night, saying hello to factory workers to whom I'd been introduced.

I found that buying rounds of drinks was a simple icebreaker, and even the poorest workers who were earning a relative wage of a few U.S. dollars a day offered to buy me local treats. They were glad to know me, something I found rather surprising, and I accepted their kindness.

Once my hotel family realized I wasn't leaving, retreating to the States having tried and failed, they treated me like a favorite cousin or uncle. George became my closest friend. He did worry about my trips to the ghetto, though. He pleaded with me to avoid certain areas.

"Dangerous," he said. "Too dangerous for White Ghost."

I was not and have never been a brawler, never one of those tough guys who looked for a fight or was keen to get in on one. But I knew that I had to gradually release my death grip on the safety of the known.

After several months, after doors seemed to be opening up for me, George introduced me to Mr. Johnson, the hotel's general manager.

"Mr. Johnson, this is Ben Stillwater. Ben, Mr. Johnson." George stood back to let us size up one another. I extended my hand. Mr. Johnson took it, gripped it lightly and said hello.

"My pleasure," I said, wondering at my own choice of words and noticing only at this moment and with some surprise that we were of equal height.

Neither of us attempted the other's language.

Mr. Johnson wore Italian suits, stood ramrod straight and rarely spoke even after our introduction. He was a nodder. Not a smiler, not by any means. And not a talker.

From then on, every day at breakfast, he would pause at my table, glance at my plate, meet my eyes, offer a lightning smile and move on. One morning I gave him a thumbs up; his smile lasted a beat longer than usual.

*****

As I was falling into my new existence, and I cannot say what triggered it, I dreamed one night of a woman standing beside my bed. My dreams so far in China were vibrant—huge people in bright colors doing extreme things. All stuff that I blamed on the food, just as Scrooge blamed the appearance of ghosts on his gruel. But you can only blame the food for just so long and for just so many dreams.

This ghost woman dream happened upon my arrival. She had a distinctly beautiful face albeit blue, dead blue, not the rapturous blue of a lover's eyes, nor the sweet-soft hue of robins' eggs. Just dead. Blue. She wore a red necklace that could as easily have been a razor thin line of blood around her neck which worried me—which was it? Was she alright? Why should I care? This was a dream. And there was a piece of jade, very round, luminous, gorgeous. Was it floating or attached to her necklace? I couldn't tell. Now she was offering it to me, holding it in her hand, her pallid hand, her fingernails blackened. She was reaching toward me, extending the jade.

I woke, of course, sweating. Oh yeah, that was a reaction to food. I wouldn't eat at Booney's, a local dive, again. I went into the bathroom and was sick. I was homesick, too, and suddenly certain that I'd made a terrible choice in coming to China, in accepting the challenge that Al had thrown down during one of our Internet chats. I said I wasn't a fighter, didn't take dares, didn't take offers to "step outside and settle" things.

I went back and sat on my bed. I watched the sun lift over Shenzhen's eastern mountains, painting my small room with deep, gold strokes. I

26

turned to look for my cell phone.

There it was on the bedside table. I could call for a taxi, rush up to any one of the airport clerks and implore her to sell me a ticket home to the US.

There was that stupid dream, that woman, cloying and clinging.

There was me, accepting the fight.

I stood up and showered and got dressed and ready for what had now become a regular routine of factory visits and networking with Shenzhen's higher-ups in manufacturing.

I thought about perfect scrambled eggs. Small comfort, but they would have to do.

Four

*T*he throbbing in my ribs subsided, and while I was still thinking I might possibly die in this alley, I was looking around for my beautiful savior. Where did she come from? Where did she go?

Then I heard Trish yelling at Napoleon, as he waved his iron stick at her. Thoughts of my dream girl vanished as I figured things were seriously going south. Then, two white vans screeched into the alley, and several men charged out with Al in the lead.

Relieved that my friend was among the "good thugs" who had arrived, I could better catch my breath.

The gangsters turned from us and faced their new threat.

A gorilla of a man, one of Al's cohorts, swaggered forward. To my surprise, his face broke into a grin, and he greeted the runt who had cracked my ribs. They began chatting like two old friends.

"What in the hell is going on?" I yelled at Al. "This son-of-a-bitch almost dismantled me, and my supposed rescuer is acting like a long lost family member. And who is the L.A. gangbanger midget? What's his problem? That little shit has done some serious damage to me," I glared at Al.

"I have no idea," Al said, sizing up my short assailant.

"And who's the guy you brought? He's a giant. And he's Napoleon's friend?" I clutched my side and sucked in oxygen. The pain radiated through my torso.

"His name is Mr. Feung. He works for me. I'm sorry this has happened to you. Are you OK?

"Oh, sure," I said, holding my ribs, and sending daggers to Mr. Two Hats. "Next time, he'll be on the short end of his stick."

Al went on to explain that Feung had been a notorious clan leader years earlier, before reforming to more "normal" employment as a law enforcer in the city of Shehnzen.

But he had more important information for me.

"Leave now. You are the gui-lao, and you will be noticed." He pointed down the alley, where my dream girl had gone, where traffic buzzed. He didn't have to tell me twice. I wanted to run but my ribs said no, so I limped along until I won the sympathy of a hellbent cab driver, climbed in not without difficulty, and collapsed, wincing, in the rear seat. I wondered if I could even find an ice pack in this city.

As the crowded sidewalks rolled by the window, I saw my reflection in the filmy glass and watched until I couldn't recognize it anymore.

Who was that girl? Why was she there? Hell, why was I here?

*****

Four x-rays and a few pain killers later, sitting with my ribs mummy-wrapped, I sipped hot tea and gazed out the window of my hotel room. The red sun spidered over the mountains, burning off the fresh morning oxygen. My phone vibrated, and I pulled it from my pocket. I saw Al's number.

"Now will you tell me what happened?" I asked, not in a warm, fuzzy way.

"It is just business, Ben, that is all." He answered. "Are your ribs OK?"

"Badly bruised, I think. Damn near splintered, if that's what you mean. I'm more pissed about what happened, and I'm not happy with your explanation," I said. "What's up with that gang? Who were these guys?"

I wanted answers. Getting ambushed in an alley was not an everyday occurrence to me. But more to the point, Al and I had been friends for years. Now, I had almost gotten my brains beat in because of him, for some unknown reason. I wanted answers. We had a business deal developing, and this was not a good beginning.

"My wife and I paid for molds. They were very, um, expensive," he hesitated a moment before continuing. "The factory owner said he was unable to finish the molds, and I wanted my money back. Trish and I

30

showed up to get the molds and some money—"

"What kind of molds, Al?"

"For toys, molds of action figures."

"Action figures? Like G.I. Joe kind of stuff?" I was trying to picture these dolls.

"No, this kind called 'Peacemakers of the World,'" Al said. "Ghandi, Martin Luther King, Nelson Mandela, and some others. Anyway, we went to get the molds, and our fifty-thousand dollars of upfront money. We got into a shoving match, and his guards forced us from the factory and told us never to return. I called the factory owner and threatened to have my collector, Mr. Feung, force the owner to return my molds along with my money. I scared him, and that is why he sent his people to scare me. Except you and Trish got caught in the middle."

He went on to explain that an organization called the "Association" was responsible.

"They lend money to a lot of business owners who want to expand or get out of trouble. They also lend to people wanting to start their own businesses. If the money is paid back, with interest, on time, all is fine. However, if not…" He let his words drift off.

I said nothing thinking that I did not want to be involved in things involving thugs and bodily harm. Then, out of nowhere, Al asked if I would attend a meeting between the Association and the factory owners.

"Why should I come? And how are the Association and the factory owners even different?" I demanded. This definitely was not on my agenda.

31

"The Association works for many factory owners, whoever pays the most. And you should come because, Mr. Feung asked that you come," he said, as if it made perfect sense. "He has never met a white ghost before, and you interest him."

"Great," I thought. The concept of "white ghost" had been a bit flattering at first. Now, I'm thinking, I would like to be less conspicuous.

"Fine," I told Al, "But if there's a fight, I'm leaving. I need to keep the rest of me intact. Got it?"

*****

On the way to the meeting, I clenched and unclenched my jaw, imagining all sorts of scenarios. "You OK?" the cab driver asked. I was also not even sure we would arrive. The driver had obviously seen our NASCAR events and was doing his best Dale Earnhardt imitation by racing across lanes and dodging buses. Speed limit? What speed limit? Lane markers, why? Stoplights? Just suggestions, really. To drive in China, you took the offensive approach—grab the lane, shove in. Or, as Al said, "Nose first goes first."

By the time we reached the hotel, I was taking deep breaths, glad to be here, but trying to stop my pounding heart. I looked up and saw that we were at the Dragon Hotel, a glowing structure of dancing LED lights, exactly eighteen long city blocks parallel to my own residence, the Bossman.

Walking into the lobby, we met Al's business partners, including Mr.

Feung.

I whispered to Al, "Mr. Feung, is he part of the Association?"

"Was. Not now."

"And he's a cop, right?"

"Yes," he said.

I stood back while they talked for a few minutes. Then we were seated in an oversized meeting room. I faced the men who had surrounded me in the alleyway, and thought of the Chinese calligraphy Trish had explained: Think. Maybe some great enlightenment would fall on me. Maybe.

I was happy to see Napoleon was absent. Secretly I hoped he'd crossed the wrong person, that someone had beaten the crap out of him, that maybe he was in a body cast now, drinking from a straw.

The clan leader had a Chairman Mao lapel pin, a nod to his belief in the power pyramid, the top-down style of government for which China was known. He smiled, and offered his hand to me. I placed my pale, sweaty palm in his, and gave a firm shake. His associates watched me, and I made sure that nothing I felt on the inside was showing on the outside. Be emotionless, I told myself.

Mr. Feung spoke and everyone fumbled for cigarettes and lighters. Smoke clouded the room with the factory owner on one side, Al on the other. I sat behind Al, and noticed a man in the middle, who I assumed was an intermediary. The meeting commenced and both sides began pulling out files stuffed with paper. It was like a deposition hearing—briefcases snapped open and closed, stacks of printouts shuffled, ashtrays began filling up. Servers brought bottled water and cleaned the ashtrays.

Then the talking began. Then the shouting.

I didn't understand what was shouted back and forth, but when the noise got too loud, the mediator would hold his hand up and demand silence. The room would settle down, then one side would begin talking until the shouting matches started again.

During the quieter moments, I leaned closer to Al and asked what was happening. He would ignore me, so I sat back in my chair and began analyzing the men who attacked us. I noticed every one, except the clan leaders, was missing one or two fingers. Was this like the Japanese Yakuza rite of body modification, a slice to affirm loyalty, or was it a penalty for disobedience?

The talking stopped. I realized they were staring at me, the White Ghost. I wondered if every American who walked these streets was regarded in this manner.

Al said they wanted to ask me some questions, that I might add an American business perspective to the problem. To buy some time and collect my thoughts, I asked Al for a bottle of water. I took a long drink and watched as the Association guys smoked and stared hard at me.

The mediator turned to me. "What do you think the worth of mold is and how would you deal with this in the United States?"

I looked around, smiled, and shrugged. I thought of the alley, the goon, the pain in my ribs and said, "With lawyers."

His forehead creased, and he didn't smile. Al translated. I was ignored. Useless American, they probably thought, why is he even here? I had my fingers and decided that ten was a good number to own, a lucky number. Ten fingers for typing emails and sudsing my shrinking hairline. Ten was perfect.

I decided that playing dumb was the best protection, so I shrugged again.

The yelling began, papers stuffed into briefcases, and the other side stood to leave.

I turned to Al and asked, "Now what?"

"Don't know."

"Is it bad, or good?"

"Don't know."

Al knew and he was choosing not to tell me. Was he protecting me or himself? I could only play dumb to a certain point, and I was not about to be a pawn in some Chinese chess game.

The mediator spoke to Al, who turned to me.

"The other clan leader wants to have drinks and dinner with you," he said.

"Who. Mr. Feung?"

"No, his friend," Al replied. I looked across the table, and for the first time, realized I was staring at a cowboy, a tall man wearing the costume of Old West heroes. Or villains.

"Why me?" All I wanted was to get out of there.

"Why? He wants to talk to you." Al made it sound like this was the most natural thing in the world.

"I don't speak Mandarin."

"I'll translate. Don't worry, I'll be here, too."

I had no choice; I had to help my friend save face. A great deal of money was at stake, and his honor was in question. I had to deal with my fear of the unknown.

The six of us spread around the table with a Lazy Susan in the middle. To the casual observer, we were preparing for a family-style dinner, except for what followed. Waiters handed out several bottles of clear liquor. Shots were poured then followed shouts of "gum-bai" as we started the universal game of machismo drinking.

I gulped the burning rice wine and slammed the shot glass down. The clan leader smiled and nodded, while Al patted my back. Then the questions began, Al translating his queries.

"Which president did you vote for in the election?"

"Neither. I don't like politics. That's why I chose to leave for China. I wanted to skip all the election nonsense and focus on my specialty, inventing products and marketing and money."

Al translated, and the clan leader nodded. He stroked his thin moustache, and I complimented his Tony Llama boots, an homage to all that is American, hard cowboy gear of black ostrich leather. To this, he grinned, patted my shoulder and in clear English said, "Clint. Clint Eastwood."

"Clint Eastwood? The actor?" I tried to figure out where this was going.

Al said, "He very much likes Western movies, with cowboys and likes Clint Eastwood best. That is his American name. Clint."

"What—is it OK if I call him that?" I asked, and Al nodded.

"Of course," he replied. The waitress brought more bottles of throat-scorching hooch, bringing on another round of shots.

I smelled my glass and knew this was the hard stuff when it burned

36

my throat. I gagged and sipped water. I looked over at Clint who was leaning back in his chair. He had an amused look in his eyes, like he thought I was a lightweight at this drinking game. He straightened up and asked me if I owned a gun.

"Yes," I said, wondering where this conversation was headed. "I practice a lot, and hunt sometimes."

His eyes widened and he asked what type of guns, what I hunted and did everyone have guns?

"Not everyone," I answered. "But many people do. Can't you own guns here?"

"No, they're illegal," he said. "The Government controls guns and controls the fear and money and people. Even police can't have guns, only military. Or the Association."

He began to give his thoughts on what he perceived to be American aggression in the Middle East, and while I did have my own thoughts, and wanted to give a truthful answer, one that would satisfy him, I decided to "plead the fifth." This was one area I did not want to enter into. China had its own record of human rights abuses, and while we could play a game of pointing out each country's faults, I didn't want to go there. Besides, the rice wine had erased my vocabulary, which was a good thing. He waved off the question, and Al continued translating the questions from Mandarin to English.

"Do you like China or U.S.A. better?" Clint mused, and he leaned back, tossed another drink back and smiled. He was challenging me. I could feel his expectation.

"I love China and the U.S. because they both offer unique things, special things," I told him. "Chinese women are beautiful and we should go sometime and drink and chase women."

He grunted his approval, smiled, and poured again. I noticed a peculiar totem, a greenish stone tile, attached to a red string hanging around Clint's neck. I complimented him on it and asked why the stone was engraved with the outline of a rooster.

"Powerful animal. Opposite of birth year, Year of Snake," he said, sitting up straight again, obviously proud of his sign. "It brings balance, and good luck."

I remembered my Chinese birth year, 1970, was the Year of the Dog, or so it had been reinforced by many years of fortune cookies and the zodiac-themed takeout menus Dad had brought home each week. So could the snake then be my opposite, too? Probably not. Hopefully not. I looked across the table at him in his black clothes and ostrich boots. Could this be my balance? A Chinese gang leader with a borrowed Hollywood name? I hoped my animal was anything but the writhing, legless, venomous snake.

I tried to respond through Al, but Clint held his hand up and said, in perfect English, "Al, you may leave. I want to speak to Ben in private, if you don't mind? Please. Thank you." He nodded his head. Al looked surprised, and left the table.

"You speak English?" I said, wondering why the subterfuge, and feeling just a bit duped.

"Yes."

"Then why was Al translating for you?" I twirled my glass, waiting for an answer.

"Why do you think so?" He smiled, and refilled our shot glasses.

I tried to wrap my mind around this, and somehow, through the fog of rice wine and cigarette fumes, I realized what had happened.

"You were challenging him?" I asked.

"Yes. Correct. A challenge."

"You wanted to know if he would translate honestly, or if he would change your words. Twist your words."

"Or your words, gui-lao."

"But he didn't lie, did he?"

"You have to ask me? You don't know already?"

I knew, and that was why I had trusted Al with so much of my business, for so long. He was an honest, decent man. I would not have gone into business with him otherwise, rib-busting aside.

Clint held out his hand, and we shook, the honest, firm grip of trust, and he said we would chase women soon. Then he left with his entourage in tow, a bizarre, dark parade of Chinese cowboys.

As I contemplated the meeting, my favorite Clint Eastwood movie, Pale Rider, ran through my mind. I considered the biblical theme of that flick: Eastwood's character was both Death and Revenge, mystical twin revelations combined into a single, powerful force of nature. He was the yin and yang of pale horse and black boots, the kind with spurs, and the ominous chant of their ringing song, as heels and spurs clicked together in deadly metronomic rhythm, hands ready to help the honest or yank the liars back to Hell.

Five

I hadn't thought of it in ages but I did now, that Halloween night, years and years ago in Missouri, one of those fall nights where the sun settles red into the Ozark foothills but you know everything is slowing, changing, evolving.

That night, the pin oak leaves swirled across the sidewalks and their rattle was comforting, not scary as it might have been on such an evening.

I was draped in a simple ghost costume, a sheet from the linen closet, and it swept the leaves behind me, dragging some of them along, scraping.

I hoped this wasn't one of Mom's good sheets, like the ones she sprinkled with lavender water and ironed. My breath was hot against the cotton, and the breeze came through the eyeholes that I had cut with pencil-box scissors. It was making my eyes water. I inhaled the soft burned scent of autumn.

My friends and I spent several hours criss-crossing the neighborhood streets and though we thought of tricks, some rather extraordinary and others inane, like the flaming bag of dog poop at someone's door, nothing came of it. We chose not to egg Samantha's big brother's car; we voted against toilet papering the school principal's trees; we gave up on ringing doorbells and running into the shadows because most of us were dressed as ghosts and couldn't run fast without tripping, or, being seen in our extra-white sheets.

No, we stuck to stuffing our pillowcases with handfuls of treats from benevolent neighbors. We oohed and aahed over the best stuff and roughly cast aside the Bible verses from Ms. Bean and the new pencils from our old kindergarten teacher, Mrs. Skarda.

We wanted, we needed, we sought absolute edible booty like chocolate bars, jellybeans, bubble gum, and even the popcorn balls that we stopped to eat on the street because our mothers would have thrown them out for fear of poison or needles.

We guffawed over our rank appetites, getting seeds and sugar stuck in our teeth, poking at it with our greedy little fingers to loosen it and ran on to the next house to see what sugary devil awaited our furious appetites.

We scattered as dusk fell.

"Well, I'm going to Mrs. Wong's house," I said.

"You're not!" said Christopher.

"You're crazy! I wouldn't go there in a thousand years," said Tim.

"I am not going with you, Ben Stillwater," said Nelly who fake shivered, then grabbed her sister's hand and they turned homeward.

"Ben, what are you thinking? She'll put a spell on you. She'll do some weird thing, give you fried dragon tongue, make you turn colors, who knows what?" This from my best friend, David.

"She never answers the door, you know," said Alice, David's sister.

"You're on your own, Benny boy. I gotta get my sister home. It's after dark and my Dad will have a fit." David and Alice turned away and started down the street.

I was alone on the street, clutching my pillowcase. This would be my hijinks, my big story to tell tomorrow at school. That I had braved the Wong house. Too bad I'd have no friends to back me up on what would happen. No witnesses if it went crazy. Actually, I could go home now and make up something about what happened.

I pressed on. The moon glowed full and clean white, and trees spiked into the purple twilight like hungry fingers. I wished that Sam, at least, was with me. Talking about best friends, Sam would be it. Because he was such a damn beautiful dog with manners to match, he used to win me extra treats when we trick-or-treated as a duo. Oh well, dogs don't live forever and it was a hard lesson learned the day Sam died. We buried him on our property. Boys don't cry.

Onward.

Mrs. Wong's house was a small, simple flat-roofed ranch with aluminum siding. A red lantern hung on the porch; it had tassles, gold paint and symbols on it. Chinese symbols, probably, since she was Chinese. I went up on the porch and realized that it was a candle in the lantern that gave off light, not a lightbulb. The candle flickered at my approach.

I knocked on the door and stepped back. Moments passed. I knocked again. Nothing. I rang the doorbell. A dull, two-note chime announced my presence. From the corner of my eye, I saw a curtain move, and I took another step back. As I was about to knock again, all pesky and full of chutzpah, the door creaked open. She stood in the doorway and said nothing.

Here was my opportunity to bolt. Or apologize. I did neither.

"Trick or treat," I said.

In the dark silence, I hoped for something—a remark, a curse, a spell, something.

I knew it was Mrs. Wong. It had to be her. No one else lived here.

"Trick or treat—do you wanna hear a joke or something?"

Still nothing.

"What did the boy say when his pooch ran away?" I said. There it was, my ridiculous joke. I waited two beats for her answer, then:

"Dog-gone!" I answered it myself.

She stepped from the shadows into the moonlight that was falling on the porch and I could see her round face. She smiled, then reached into her pocket and I thought that this would be the moment, the very moment when I would be chastised or charmed or made to disappear by her magic.

Of course I was wrong. She now held something in her hand.

"What year were you born?"

"1970, Mrs. Wong. I just turned twelve last week. My dad says this is my last year to trick-or-treat. He says I'm probably a little too old for this now." I would have talked and talked if it would make her smile and not do away with me for invading her porch and privacy.

"1970. That was a Year of the Dog, and that is very good. That is very good luck to be born in that year."

She picked through the envelopes she held in her hand, and then slipped one of them into my pillowcase. There in the moonlight, I would swear, as I later did many times, that glitter and colorful sparks followed that envelope into my pillowcase, that I heard it nestle itself among the wrapped candies already jumbled within.

She nodded again and pointed to my bag. Her English was perfect though smacked of the slightest accent; I could hear it. And I loved it.

"You are Ben Stillwater, right?"

"Yes." How did she know? She did have magic.

"You are a very good ghost, but not very frightening," she said.

"Thank you," I said though I was a tad disappointed. Should I have been scarier? Did she want me to be? I thanked her again, now having said it twice like a dork, and I left.

On the way home I was tempted to pull the envelope from my sack and examine it, but I could feel her eyes on my back, or so I thought. I walked faster and faster. I pulled the sheet over my head, tucked it under my arm and began to run.

*****

Alone in my bedroom, I dumped the contents of the bag on my bed and then set about the business of separating everything. The candy went into two different piles; the first was stuff to keep, like anything chocolate and also any brand of gum which I would later cram into my mouth, several pieces at a time. And the second pile was "everything else," stuff I would share or give away. Oh, keep the sweet sours. Oh, and the chewy chocolate rolls.

I was merely prolonging the suspense about the envelope. I'd be the lucky one for having braved ringing her doorbell. I saw that it had a red ribbon attached to it and attached to that, a charm.

I picked it up. The charm was of a dog, a little gold dog. "Year of the Dog, very lucky," she had said. I gave the charm a yank, it came free of the ribbon and I slipped it into my pocket. I already had a plan for that.

Now, the envelope. Was there a curse inside? Or a spell? Or, a fortune? Yes, yes, a fortune?

Inside was a postcard of a village and in the foreground, two young women, maybe twin sisters, holding hands with a little girl. They were all dressed in pink, sitting on a bench. Something was written along the bottom of the card, perhaps the title of the picture? I couldn't tell; it seemed to be Chinese characters. There was nothing on the back of the card. I tossed it aside. What did I care about that?

I was going to put the dog charm in my cigar box vault which I retrieved from my closet shelf. I opened the lid, glanced at its contents, stuff I'd been saving since I was really little and noticed a yellowed bit of paper. What was this? I picked it out of the marbles and pebbles and read it aloud:

The Year of the Dog: If you were born in the Year of the Dog (1922, 1934, 1946, 1958, 1970) you keep secrets well, may have great wealth but will not be money-driven, can be emotionless and distant, will make a good leader, can be selfish and stubborn, are compatible with those born in the year of the tiger, horse, or rabbit.

Your fortune: Destiny lies beyond your fear.

None of it had made sense when my mother first read it aloud to me from my first fortune cookie from the restaurant on Edward Street. And it made no sense now. Except the Year of the Dog part. That was kind of a coincidence.

I refolded the fortune, shoved it into the cigar box along with the dog charm. I was twelve. This was all important stuff.

As for the postcard, yeah would make a good bookmark, that is, if I, the magnificent and very brave Ben Stillwater who went to Mrs. Wong's on Halloween, ever wanted to read a book.

I lay on my bed, ate three miniature boxes of chocolate-covered caramels and thought about the story I would tell tomorrow at school.

Six

I. pulled a thin, red cotton sweater over my head, and felt a loose trail of yarn hanging from my left sleeve. I tugged, unraveled a bit of it, swore, yanked the thing back over my head and threw it at my closet. I almost wished I had a costume to wear, even if the locals didn't understand the concept of Halloween.

Al arrived to pick me up for our journey to the local hotspot, a karaoke bar called "Jade." I tried not to let my nerves give me away. The fact I couldn't sing a note to save my life kept me away from most karaoke bars, plus I just wanted to keep a low profile. I was here for business. I didn't want to get involved with any perceived underbelly of Shenzhen. Molds, whatever, just let me go with the Eastern flow.

"Happy one year in China!" Al crowed, looking over his shoulder at traffic before pulling out into the flow.

"Yep. One year, and I'm still alive," I replied, and laughed.

"Jade is certainly popular here. Even naming bars after it," I remarked just to make conversation.

"Jade," Al said, "is very valuable."

"I know," I replied, "they sell the stuff in the U.S."

"But did you know jade isn't always green?"

"Sure it is." I clutched my seatbelt, as Al punched the accelerator and skinned past a line of delivery trucks. Watch your pucker muscle, my Dad used to say, when we'd ride the tummy-ticklers on backwoods roads.

"No. Jade is green, milky-green, and sometimes brown," Al replied.

"I thought jade meant green," I said.

"I saw the jade ship in the lobby of the Bossman and it's beautiful. And it's *very* green."

"The expensive jade is green, but translucent," Al said, "and is very rare."

The ghost had been wearing a jade necklace. A perfect circle, tied with red string. And it was green, not brown. Why would a ghost wear jewelry?

My stomach tightened at the memory. I wanted to ask Al to turn around. Maybe I should stay in for the evening. Drink some of that nasty pink stomach med, snack on a cup of noodles, and call it a night.

Jade announced itself with a large green neon sign trying to fit in with the other neon signs shouting out other clubs along the crowded street.

48

Al wheeled the car to a curb, and a valet ran up to his window. He tossed him the keys, and we walked into the lavish club. Men and women of all shapes and sizes stood elbow to elbow, laughing with forced animation. Would they find love tonight? Even for a little while?

We were ushered to a private room lined with oversized couches. An enormous lacquer table piled with plates of fruits and nuts stood in the center. Plastic buckets of Tsingtao sat under the table, and mammoth TV screens hung on three walls. The garbled noise of American music sung out of tune in drunken gibberish rose above the din.

We sank down on a garish red couch and signaled a waiter. While we waited, we began discussing our project.

"This is going to be great," Al said, leaning in toward me. "I will make these numbers work, don't worry."

The waiter arrived and set our drinks on the small table.

"Come on," I slapped Al's arm. "We're here, and we're going to have a good time. A toast to our venture!"

I raised my glass and his met mine with a solid clink. We smiled and knocked back the first drink. Having heard the horror stories of American businessmen, weakened with drinks then sleeping with prostitutes, I had control. I wasn't some yahoo on a business jaunt, treating this country like an Asian Vegas playground. I had worked too long and too hard to reach this point, and I wasn't about to lose my cool.

Hours later, there I was yelling "gum-bai!" at the top of my lungs, slamming beer after Chinese beer. Through an alcohol fog, I saw a decanter of cola-colored liquid sitting in front of me. I collected the stout glass jug, and rolled the label over. Underneath a confusion of Chinese characters I read the English translation: deer penis, deer antler, snakeskin, turtle, scorpion. I groaned. No way would I put this concoction in my body. No way.

"Mr. Stillwater, you like?" A sandpapery hand brushed my cheek. I turned to see a Picasso of puckered red lips and piles of black hair. The old woman's face was a wash of chlorine white, a moon set upon an ebony stage. A tiny smirk pulled at her cheeks. "You like, or not?"

Evidently, she was trying to entice me to drink this. No, I thought, it's nasty and I can't believe that anyone would intentionally drink this! But, in an alcohol-induced fog, I nodded. She poured a shot.

"Gum-bai!" she hollered, and she downed the ounce of liquor then poured another, balancing the foul drink under my nose.

I held the heavy glass and jokingly pinched my nose and tossed it back. "Gum-bai!" I yelled, swallowing the thick liquid in one gulp. I continued to hold my breath, grinning all the while until she smiled, and drifted away like some miniature phantom, spidery and quiet and cold. I exhaled with a whoosh, and breathed deep, expelling any aftertaste. I coughed and turned to Al.

"Who was that woman?" I asked.

"The Madame."

"The what?" I struggled to hear as the din in the club grew louder and louder.

"The Madame," he yelled. "She gives the girls."

"Gives the girls? I don't understand." But I soon would.

She returned later and asked me if I wanted to choose a girl. This was a first for me, and while I didn't want to appear under appreciative, the whole concept did not sit well. For lack of knowing how to extricate myself from the situation, I just said, "I don't know." In minutes, she produced two skinny twenty-somethings dressed in tight-fitting spandex sequined with alarming numbers of rhinestones.

"Speak English!" She gave each girl a gentle shove in my direction, and one looked into my eyes.

"Wall. Eye. Knee." The girls repeated each word with precision, and the Madame rolled her eyes and walked away.

"What are they talking about?" I asked Al.

"They said they love you," he answered with a wide grin. "Good luck!"

My cheeks burned and while I wanted to make some kind of conversation, my tongue was frozen. The girls moved to sit on my lap. What to think? What to do? My mind raced, as I had never had the pleasure (or displeasure, I wasn't sure) of two escorts shoved onto my lap. The younger version of myself mentally slapped me. I stood and asked the girls if they would like to play dice. The absence of response was answer enough, and I moved to the table where my factory associates were in heated talks over beers, while cubes of bone were shaken and tossed onto the table.

"What's the bet?" I asked Al.

"Nothing, just win or if you lose, slam a beer."

And so there I was, the White Ghost cracking the dice across the black felt table. Winning, losing, I didn't really care. I was tossing rice beer down my throat, and the girls just stood and watched and drank along with me, each with either a hand on my waist or a tepid beer. I knew what I was supposed to do with them, and that this was what they expected. But I didn't have to feel right about it, even through my beer-fog.

Later that night, I sat on my hotel bed with the two naked girls. They asked me to drink and I did. We showered, the three of us, our bodies touching, crowded in the small cubicle. I stood motionless and closed my eyes, not thinking, not caring how I got here, while they soaped me, the warm water, and the feel of their hands, dancing like feathers over my body, drove away any remaining feelings of guilt.

They lay on either side of me and I watched as their petite chests rose and fell under the white cotton sheets. Then I curled into a fetal ball and fell deep into my dreams. Drapery sheers billowed through the open window, and the moon skipped behind a tight scrum of midnight clouds. A woman stood at the window, and she wore fire stilettos and her backless dress, the color of rich cream, revealed a pattern of Chinese tattoos, a column of black characters from neck to waist. In my dream, I could translate each stark icon:

Earth

Air

Fire

Water

The four elementals painted on her back. The tattoos blurred and she turned to me. A red string tightly wound her neck like a blood-rope, and she beckoned to me.

Half-naked and freezing, I rose from the bed and walked to her. She held her hand for me to take. I reached for her, and as my hand nearly touched hers, she melted into the air and disappeared into the night.

I awoke, standing at the open window, with the morning sun warming my pale skin. I turned, half-expecting the ghost behind me, but there was only the tangled mass of bedclothes and skin.

I watched the girls sleep. Their pink fingernails were the color of some cheerful cupcake, and butterflies had been temporarily tattooed their arms, but the palette of light ink had been rubbed into colorful webs of partial antennae and tail wings from a night of vigorous contact. I marveled at their petite features, the thin slope of nose and soft cheeks arced into the short straight manes of black hair.

Red and gold panties, bras and form-fitting skirts had fallen to the floor. I did not remember that, and I walked into the bathroom, trying to retrieve the memory out of respect for them.

I showered, stepped out and looked in the mirror while I brushed my teeth. Cool hands began caressing my back. I looked down and saw pink-tipped nails slipping under my arms, finding my chest, entangling themselves in my hair and finding my nipples.

Looking up into the mirror, I saw her reflection. I froze, and wondered if I was only dreaming of the ghost again, but with a pink fingernail to her lips and shushing, I knew this was no dream. She smoothed her hand around to my waist, moved downward and began to caress me. Her mouth curved into a quick, sly smile-smirk. I moved to her, and she spoke the single bit of English she knew.

"Thank you."

"Why are you thanking me?" I was taken aback by what she said. Did she know what she was saying? Or was this just what she had been taught?

Her blank eyes didn't answer. I felt her hands move downward and grasp me. In the light of a fresh day, without the dark landscape of the karaoke bar, shame gnawed at me, along with the animal wine in my stomach. I looked into the mirror and saw the fuzzy whiteness of my skin, and how easily it eclipsed her petite frame.

God help me, I thought, I have a Chinese call girl thanking me for counterfeit intimacy, and another sleeping in my bed. Anger and embarrassment built up in me for getting drunk, for allowing the currency of sexual favor, but most of all, for becoming the caricature of the Western Businessman. I loathed myself for it.

She led me back to the bed, and I surrendered any remaining vestiges of guilt.

The TV flickered, its dull glow disappearing in the morning sunlight. While European rugby teams criss-crossed a field in mute resolution, I lay between two prostitutes, caught in a way of life that would probably kill their young souls (or lives!) in a few years. And the shame I felt for helping that happen made me swear that never again would I get caught up in the macho business charade.

My thoughts then went to business and money, of intimate connections and my growing need to feel safe, part of a team, of something bigger, stronger, and more secure. I thought of home. But was that the place? I had committed to make my path here, to do the things I wanted to do. Somewhere, there was a compromise.

I would find it.

Seven

I could tell the masseuse was shy to touch me. I could tell by the way she brushed her hands over my legs first before beginning a vigorous rub. "Very hairy," she said. But I was wrong. I found out afterward from George that she was blind.

She kneaded my calf and I winced but she kept at it until I relaxed, then took up the other one and we went through the same tensing, relaxing exercise. Next my heels. When she pressed the first one with a rather amazing strength, I grunted. "It's your stomach. You have a problem there," she said.

And she was right. I had been eating rather indiscriminately in the small ghetto restaurants. Something likely in one of them had begun to affect my digestive system.

"You relax. I can work this out." I did not complain. I was open to any natural healing and any improvement in my digestion. She worked and worked and time passed; I couldn't say how much, but George was on the other table and I could hear his conversation from time to time with his masseuse. It was pleasant and soothing in the room. I was learning to relax.

The masseuse pulled on the hair on my arms and tittered again.

"George, why is she laughing?" I was too relaxed to try out my Mandarin and ask her myself.

"It's OK, Ben. It's probably because you are so hairy. She has never encountered so much hair."

"Oh, I...I..."

"It's OK, Ben. Relax and be here." I couldn't tell if he was giving me a command to be in the moment or if his English was just a bit broken, though I suspected it was the former.

So I took his advice and put myself in the moment.

*****

Later that evening, as the air cooled and the streets came to life, George invited me to meet some of his factory owner friends. We took a taxi to a bar and following introductions all around, we were downing shots of rice wine and dark liquor, and sharing war stories about factories and manufacturing. George interpreted.

"Gum bai!" We yelled it out before each shot, one after the other, and my hands became greasy with stuffing seafood kongee into my mouth.

Minutes, hours later, I fumbled my way to the men's room. Washing up, I smiled and talked to myself in the mirror, always a sign that I was drunk, gonzo. As always in public facilities, there were no paper towels or hand dryers. I shook my hands and was about to wipe them on my jeans as I entered the long hallway back into the bar.

And there she was, offering her starched white shirttails for me to dry my hands. I stood stock still looking at her. How drunk was I? This was the woman with the delicate hands and the beautiful round moon-face, my savior who had been in the alley that night.

"Uh, no thanks. I'll use my shirt, er, my jeans, thankyouverymuch," I said but she grabbed my hands, wrapped her shirt around them anyway and rubbed them slowly, then lifted my hands to her lips and kissed them, then turned and walked away. My dull-witted thanks lost in the noise of the bar.

"Thank you. Hey, thanks! Hey, who are you?" Ah, the profound wit and conversation of the very drunk but enamored man. "You saved me that night!" I yelled to no one in particular though several people turned to stare at me, then returned to their drinking.

*****

Later, in a conscious moment or maybe not so conscious, I begged George for information about her. He knew very little though he had seen her at the restaurant often enough and believed she might know a little English. I was intrigued; I was enamored, damn, I really liked this girl. Please, please would he ask her if she would join all of us in a game of ping-pong or pool sometime?

*****

A week later, we had a date. Her name was Xiao, pronounced "shall." She worked twelve-hour shifts at a restaurant, a high-end establishment well beyond the manufacturing district.

Xiao did not come alone; she brought Grace, a friend. That was fine. I had George as my "second" or rather, as my wingman.

Xiao accepted my offer of ping-pong. She would be glad to have me show her the game. I noticed that she had a remarkably good grasp on the racquet and could twirl it. Such showiness. But could she play the game?

I served. She returned the ball with a slam to my face.

OK, this was not a girl like the other Chinese I had met. Yes, she wore the demure face, was willing to bow and to dry the White Ghost's hands, but there was steeliness here, something sharp, experienced, maybe dangerous.

I had to know this beautiful woman. I had to know her story.

Another week passed and she deigned to meet me for dinner. Again, with Grace. Again, with George. But I brought along a pair of Chinese/English translation books nevertheless. I counted to ten in Mandarin for Xiao, looking for encouragement. Instead I got:

"Do you have a family?"

"Yes."

"Do you have a brother?" she asked.

"Yes." My voice was loud, and I nodded. She would understand that.

"Do you have a sister?" she asked.

"No, no sister. How do you say bill?" I asked, turning to George. I wanted to pay the damn bill. How could she be so interested in my family-line up this early in the game? We were having separate conversations if you wanted to call them that.

"Ben, thank you for the date. Thank you for the dinner. I have to leave for work."

Dammit, all this time, I had been stumbling over words in her language only to find she could speak mine. And now she was leaving.

"So, you speak very good English."

"Yes. And so do you." She stood. I stood, too. There was a moment before I leaned toward her and offered the clumsy hug familiar to adolescents.

She backed away, her eyes suddenly wide. I quickly offered my hand instead. She accepted with the lightest touch, grazing my skin with her fingertips. Then she drifted out into the humid night of factory and machine, into the teeming humanity pouring through the city, gone, lost in the crowd. She really had the disappearing act down nicely.

George smiled and tugged at my shoulder. "Traditional Chinese women do not hug unless it's family," he said.

"Oh. Yeah. Well, I thought she didn't like me."

"She likes you, or she would not have met with you."

"But she brought a friend. And didn't stay long."

"Be patient. You are gui-lao, and she does not know you. Be

patient."

*****

We double-dated for several weeks until my patience earned me time alone with Xiao. We chose to stumble through a meal together until I could finally finagle a ping-pong rematch with her.

She paid for dinner. I was foiled there but as we left the restaurant, I grabbed her hand. She registered surprise, but didn't pull her hand away, not immediately.

We headed to the bar to play. On the way, she pulled out her cell. I panicked, wondering if she was hoping to get out of our date. Maybe she would make up an excuse like having to meet a friend or having to go to work because it was busy. I had done it myself many times in my dating past.

Xiao hung up, smiling. We kept walking. Good, she had conjured no quick escape. We remained alone together. And again she was the consummate ping-pong player, slamming the ball into my chest again and again. We retired to the bar and ordered hot green tea. Her phone rang and after a brief conversation with someone, she looked at me.

"I have to go to work. I want to say goodbye. Forever," she said.

"Forever? What? You mean you don't want to see me again?"

She shook her head. "No, I want to say goodbye. Forever. Goodbye." And she turned away.

"I don't understand. Why?"

She quickly produced her cell phone, and made a call. She spoke

60

into the phone, her forehead a serious furrow, and then she brightened and looked at me.

"I mean, see you tomorrow! See, my English is not always so good. I have things to learn." She gave me a quick hug and left. A hug. Oh, we were making progress. I regretted not walking her to work, and wanted to call her but headed back to the Bossman Hotel. I knew it was time to start putting down roots here. I needed to find a place to call my own, an apartment. I had to be self-sufficient, without the comforts of a hotel chef and cleaning girls.

As soon as I was in the door, someone was pounding on it. It was Xiao. She smiled and hugged me and said, "I'll try this again, but will say it better. Goodbye, see you tomorrow."

I thought my heart would pound out of my chest.

Eight

$\mathcal{I}$n my cement tower, I watched the night unfold, and once again, the need to find a more permanent residence dominated my thoughts. I knew I would be staying in China indefinitely, and if I was indeed going to make a commitment, whether business, personal, or both, I had to put down roots somewhere, sometime, and it might as well be now.

I spent my days visiting factories and calling potential buyers. It looked as if Al's and my business deal with the solar power trains was going to fly. We just had to nail down a few more odds and ends, and a major one was engineering the best train design. That looked like it was about to happen.

So, I was proficient in business, but how could I find an apartment, read the classifieds, when the only Chinese script I could read were the numbers 1 through 10? Should I call a real estate agent? What would an apartment cost? Would it have a western toilet, or the communal floor hole common to the typical local residences?

I knew apartments were small, generally one room, but at least I could make it our own. "Our." The word had a nice ring to it. Xiao was moving in with me. I wanted her to move in with me.

We had been dating for well over three months. I wanted to be with her all the time. Our work schedules were so fractured. She worked from 6 p.m. to 6 a.m. I worked from 8 a.m. to maybe 4 p.m. or 5 p.m. If we were in the same place, we could have more time together. Her rare days away from work became mini-vacations through the city, as she helped me with my Mandarin. We ate dim sum at breakfast, shopped for dinner at the market, and found numerous jigsaw pathways through Central Park, pausing to watch the dozens of badminton players there.

I thought of her perfect face, her fragile beauty masking resiliency and power. There was a reason to stay, and it wasn't just business and money. Our budding relationship was the balance in my own personal battle with language, culture, and soon, as I was to find out, the Chinese Mafia. I was in China, dating a girl I could barely communicate with, and maybe, just maybe, I was falling in love.

I got the cell phone from the bedside table and called Al. His phone was cutting out, and I redialed several times, until the connection held. Finally, he answered.

"I need to find a place, Al. I need something more permanent. If I'm going to be here for awhile, I want something that might pass for home, not a stopover." My words spilled out within seconds, as if I feared not saying them quickly would cause them to disappear.

"Good. I will call Trish and she will be able to help," he said. "This should be no problem. Let me call you back."

I closed my phone and sank back into my firm pillow. Just like that, I'm going to settle into this crazy city of noise, pollution, and gangsters. Yes, I thought, just like that.

Later, Trish called, like Al said.

"So, you want to move now?" she asked.

I told her I needed an apartment, a place to call my own, even if it wasn't. I needed more permanence than where I was staying now. I had gotten close to George, Mr. Johnson, and the rest of the staff who tried mightily to please me, but it was time to move on.

"I'll pick you up tomorrow afternoon," she said. "I'll have a list of places you might like."

Over the next two weeks, I looked at every feasible type of apartment I could afford, most smaller than my parents' living room back in Missouri. Trish was getting exasperated with what she saw as my extreme pickiness.

"You're not going to find a place like home," she said one evening after an afternoon of futile searching. "This is how it is here. We don't have large apartments. We have to fit too many people in small spaces."

"I know," I sighed, thinking about my options, which were few.

I made a pledge that the next day that I would keep an open mind and lower the bar. My positive thinking must have worked because the first one Trish and I saw in the morning called to me. It wasn't that far from the hotel, and while it wasn't much bigger than the hotel room I had now, it offered a bit more space and character.

It had two rooms, one with a couch, an upholstered chair, and a desk and chair; the other was a bedroom. Then there was the postage-stamp bathroom that afforded a modicum of privacy. The kitchen was a galley with a small stove and refrigerator taking up most of one wall.

The apartment did, however, feature a patio that opened to the cacophony and exhaust fumes from the congested street sixteen floors below. But it gave me a feeling of sanctuary. Xiao would be happy.

The day I moved my belongings, I sought out Mr. Johnson. He had become my confidant. Maybe a better, modern word was mentor. I felt the need to tell him that although I was moving, I would be close and hoped to continue tea together at the hotel restaurant. I would miss our conversations about Chinese history and culture, talks that helped me to feel less alien here. I would miss our friendship.

I found him in the hall, explained that I was moving, but that I would be in touch. He smiled and gave a slight bow. I bent awkwardly, still uncomfortable with the custom. But I would learn.

Nine

$\mathcal{I}$ was anxious to move from the hotel and begin a routine in my own place, with no service or servers. I was on my own to cope with cooking and cleaning (to some small extent) and whatever small repairs or pleasures were to be had.

But there was a hitch. A cultural hitch, and certainly one on which I chose not to dwell. It was this: Before I could spend my first of many nights in the new apartment, apparently my new landlord had to do so, first. With his wife. The two of them. In the biblical sense.

For God's sake, I thought. I was certainly capable of breaking in the place myself but apparently unmarried coupling did not chase away demons. Custom would have it that the landlord and his spouse, from the realm of my bed, would cleanse the dwelling space of bad spirits and negative energy. Any bad luck would then go away. It is a custom, they said.

Well, it was my custom to move into a new place, throw clean sheets on the bed, cast my cares to the wind, as in leaving everything still packed, and climb into the bed and into the arms of Morpheus. And this time, I wanted to sleep the sleep of a man who has just moved everything he owns in the Eastern hemisphere from a hotel room into a two-room apartment.

But I didn't say that. No. Someone else's sleep and sperm and dreams were required for cleansing purposes. Curious. Maybe I should strive to be a landlord and sleep around in my own building so to speak.

Xiao was coming with me, though. She was moving in with me. Today was moving day.

My God. Xiao at last.

Maybe to prolong our excitement, we were going shopping first, then would haul our loot back to our "new" three rooms. We were in pursuit of sheets, cleaning stuff, and groceries. We just wanted to shop. We had energy to burn. There had been so much waiting.

Xiao picked me up early that brilliant Saturday morning, knocking and slapping on my hotel door, calling my name in all her excitement. Though we had sometimes camped out at Xiao's place, despite her chest-of-drawers-size apartment, I had never pushed her to any sexual commitment. Though we were past hugging, which still was not Xiao's forte, our very few overnights together would, by American standards, be called platonic. I was secretly glad.

This morning, Xiao was all wound up, over the top in fact, about shopping with her White Ghost. She chattered on and on in the taxi and I caught the words "towels" and "blankets" and listened to her lists of foodstuffs. She clapped her hands and patted my knees as the cab driver careened down a busy street.

"Happy?"

"Yes, Xiao—I am happy. And excited to move into the new apartment. With you."

"Where do you want to go now?"

"We're going to Wal-Mart. I heard there's a huge Wal-Mart outside of Shenhzen. Do you know about it?"

She frowned.

"You know, Wal-Mart." I was vaguely surprised she didn't understand what I was saying.

"Shenma?" she said, the Chinese equivalent of "What?"

I pronounced it again, drawing out the two syllables, and even added a few extra ones. Wasn't Wal-Mart a fairly typical store, worldwide?

"What are you doing?" she said as I pulled out my cell phone.

"Calling Al. He can translate." It was an old habit by now to call him. When he picked up, I got quickly to the point.

"Al, this is Ben. Have you been to Wal-Mart?"

"No."

"Do you know what store I am talking about?"

"No."

"Wal-Mart. The big shopping place. Blue sign. W-A-L-M-A-R-T."

"OK, yes, yes. I know it."

I suspected he was being respectful and didn't really know what I wanted.

"Al, would you explain to Xiao where I want to go?"

"Sure."

I handed the phone over to her, and after a five-minute conversation, she snapped it shut and looked even more confused. "I don't understand," she said softly in Mandarin.

"Don't worry. The taxi driver knows. I just asked him. It's about five miles. " Again, I got a confused look from Xiao. We sat in silence until suddenly, Xiao was pointing and yelling "Oh! Wall R Mart! You mean Wall R Mart!" as the big blue letters loomed into view.

"That's what I said!"

"No, you said a different thing. Not the same, but I understand." She shook her hair, plucked at her sleeves, and smoothed her skirt.

We joined the swarms of people going in and out of the store. Factory workers, off the clock after long shifts, crowded the monstrous, three-story store. Xiao said there was nightly entertainment, fashion shows, product demonstrations, and singing to attract customers.

"They want the people's money," she said. "But most spend only around 40 RMB. That is about four dollars."

It was impossible to move without bumping into someone. We watched the crowd gathered around a juicer demo as we took the escalator to the second floor. Here, people were standing in awe of flat-screen TVs and tech-gear demonstrations. They played with all sorts of game units, digital cameras, stereos, and apparently anything they could touch. These were luxury items—I wondered how many people would actually be purchasing anything.

We wandered a bit, getting our bearings. A store employee was dispersing a crowd of gawkers to make room for buyers. A strange job, I thought. But suddenly I felt like everyone's eyes were on us. In fact, they parted to let us through. Xiao whispered that they were judging her, because she was a Chinese with a Western man.

I didn't like it, I was a little nervous nearly to the point of irritation with the outright staring. I took Xiao's arm, and marched past the blenders, camcorders, and electric brooms until we entered the sanctuary of the book department. Even here, shoppers stood shoulder to shoulder in aisle upon aisle of books. Children lay on the concrete floor, chins in their hands, reading books they had propped open. I realized this was a library; akin to our huge bookstore cafes back in the states, just not as nicely appointed. The kids didn't care. They were quiet, enchanted. I turned to Xiao to point out a remarkable little kid who was reading aloud to her baby sister, but Xiao was gone.

*****

It took me awhile to find her. I had to stop and think what might lure her. Yes, there she was in the beauty department, hovering over soaps and lotions and makeup whose aisles were nearly as prodigious as those in the book department.

She smiled up at me, explaining that she might buy what the "talk" is, the products that her group of friends purchased. She also had a Cosmopolitan magazine in her hand. Curious, I asked why she wanted it.

"To look like American girl," she said.

"What? You're beautiful. I don't want an American girl, I want you."

"Why?"

"Why, what?"

"Why do you want me when you have so many Chinese girls to date?"

"Well, why do you like me, when there are so many Chinese men to date?"

She paused, then looked right at me. "Love is love. That is why I am here. With you. So why do you like me?"

This was one of those conversations in which women are adept. Not men. We don't like to think fast about emotion on our feet. And I did not want to be trapped into the "love" word while standing in Wal-Mart. I did not want this conversation here. But Xiao was direct, and I felt compelled to be just as brave.

"You are pure and honest, Xiao. You have a big heart. You don't seem to have a checklist of expectations like most women."

She seemed content with that, but I wasn't sure if she understood what I had said, and it was impossible to read her face.

Still clutching the magazine, she said, "I like the U.S.A. because of you, Ben. I want to meet your family, your mother, everyone who knows you. I love China because of family, my friends, our tradition, even our food. I love the way of life I know, but I want to embrace yours, too, like I embrace you."

This was not the time to give her some more truths as we stood getting jostled by makeup-mad shoppers and pestered by sales clerks who were assigned aisles to parade and assist. "No, thank you," I kept saying to them as I considered telling Xiao that in the U.S., a person can drink tap water straight from the faucet, can eat fruit and vegetables without cooking them to kill the germs, can revel in miles and acres of personal space and fresh air and shopping malls and convenience.

Plucked from Shenzhen and its surroundings, the simple country girl in front of me would miss her family, her hometown, her ways, the sound of her language, the duality of the stink and fragrance of China.

And I was a country boy at heart. Even with my big ideas and my leap of faith, my family and friends were the most important part of my life. I would bring Xiao home, she could sample my lifestyle, and I could measure her reactions and she could return to Shenzhen if it didn't work out. Was I ready?

Would this be like my past relationships, moments of serenity interrupted by the hard reality of my work schedule, the necessary space I needed to create and market my products? How many times had women told me that I was more in love with making money?

We were out of the makeup and into the jewelry. And there, something caught my eye. It was a pendant on which dangled a perfect circle of jade and it matched perfectly the one I had seen on the ghost.

"You like it?" Xiao said.

"I do. I don't know why, but I really like it." I was not going to relate my ghost story.

"You should buy it, Ben."

"What? No. I don't want it. Anyway, we need to shop. Enough browsing. We have a lot to do."

I found an empty shopping basket (lucky me) and began purposeful purchases that included an inexpensive DVD player, and a five-gallon water dispenser, with both hot and cold taps. Xiao would learn to cook with purified water, a necessity here. No more of the rancid stuff that flowed from canals into the city's water system.

Of course I bought her the makeup she'd been clutching as well as shampoo, soap, and towels, which she chose with little deliberation. Our basket was filling quickly. I was sweaty, nearly feverish with the staring shoppers, the press of them, the amount of time it took to work our way from counter to counter and department to department. I wasn't used to shopping this way, there were special rules here, and I was ready to leave.

Stopped by a guard, we were told that our DVD must be paid for in its own department, as with the bath and beauty supplies and we would be given receipts to then show the guards on each level of the store. I was ready to call it a day, even the malls of American make me crazy, but suddenly, springing up like an oasis, there was the food department. Familiar food!

I nearly dragged Xiao along, holding her hand under mine on the handle of the basket. She skipped to keep up with me. Cola. Pretzels. Chocolate. Cream-filled cookies. Oh, precious junk food, stuff I never bought back home, but now just the sight of its familiar packaging comforted me. I had to have it all. I picked up a half dozen frozen pizzas, several bags of cookies, and a restaurant-size container of pretzels.

The frozen food section was an eye-opener—there was freezer chest after chest of seafood dumped into massive bins without packaging. People grabbed bags from a dispenser and loaded them with the legs, claws, whole fish and lots of unrecognizables.

Xiao and I filed into the checkout lane, one of at least twenty of them. People were noisy, chattering, excited; surprisingly, most held only one or two items. Good. This wouldn't take long after all.

Xiao said most of them purchased only basic needs items, spending 30 to 50 RMB, which was approximately $3 or $5 in the U.S.

"Why?" I knew a lot of the younger people in here were earning in one week what their families out in the country were earning in a year.

The youth had money.

"Because there is no room to store much," she said. "Most people shop every day for dinner and the basic necessities. Toys are scarce, because there is no room to store them, either. Wardrobes and shoes are kept to a minimum for the same reason."

I didn't say so aloud, but I liked that idea. Less is more. Surely it had an inherent lesson to be applied. I would have to use this in my business dealings and manufacturing as well. I elbowed her and whispered, "They are staring again."

Xiao pointed to our cart, nearly overflowing with products. "That's why," she said, smiling at everyone around her.

So now it was my blatant consumption, not my white skin that was obvious. Dammit. I suddenly felt greedy and my cheeks burned. Hey, I'm moving in with this beautiful woman, I wanted to shout at them. But I kept my yap shut, paid the 500 RMB, and pushed our cart toward the exit.

Four employees stopped us to check our receipt. But the crowds, the heat, the staring, my overkill on purchases flipped a switch; I was annoyed, no, furious and snatched back my receipts when they were done. "Why would I steal anything, why should I be treated like a crook? You saw me pay!" I said.

They replied with blank stares. Thank God. I was not exactly on board the peace train here with my outburst. They were just doing their jobs.

Outside, as Xiao snatched worried glances at me, I snagged a taxi, and loaded our things into the trunk, ignoring the cab driver's look of surprise and enthusiastic assistance. Jeez, these people liked to touch things. But weren't into hugging. Go figure.

I was silent during the ride. Xiao was wise. "Be patient, Ben," she said, "Find peace. You will be stronger without frustration and anger. Without so much negative emotion, you can overcome fear."

What did she know of my fear, of my struggle to survive here, to prosper, to understand her and how I felt about her? I remained quiet but held her hand with both of mine.

I paid the cabbie, we grabbed our haul from the trunk and rode the elevator in silence. She unlocked the security gate and front door; her hands were shaking and she had a little trouble with the keys that I had pressed into her hand moments ago in the taxi. Mine were probably shaking, too.

Inside our apartment, which looked pristine in its near emptiness, Xiao slid her arms around my neck, kissed me lightly and said she would deal with the shopping bags. I was anxious to get the rest of our stuff moved in; Al and Trish were bringing the rest later. Maybe they could bring a bit of zen for me, as well.

I wanted to check my emails, get on the phone. But for now, I could wave those tasks away as both impossible and silly. I walked across the small living room to stare out the window at the late afternoon.

The weather was being kind; the neighborhood had a certain shine to it and the sounds that drifted up to the sixteenth were sweet, like summer. Xiao was running back and forth between our galley-size kitchen and the bathroom, I supposed, stashing stuff, getting organized. I have always admired a woman's ability to create a home. I thought of my mother's house, of my friend Anne again.

There was a third room in this apartment, it would be my office. Standing there in the middle of the room, I extended my arms and could nearly touch the walls. OK, all I needed in here was a desk and my laptop.

"Shall I make dinner?" Xiao said as I walked back into the kitchen.

She was shoving the pizza boxes into the small freezer of the very small fridge.

"Yes. But not now."

I put my hands on her shoulders and smiled down at her. I could feel her pulse in that delicate throat and leaned in to kiss her. She laughed softly but did not pull away.

"Wait, I have something for you," she said. She took something from her pocket. "Here. This is for you. For you to wear." She pressed a small, round object into my hand. It was the red string necklace from which dangled the jade circle.

"You said you liked the necklace, Ben, at Wall-R-Mart, right?"

"I did." I closed my eyes for a second, feeling the jade's smooth coolness in my palm.

"Thank you, Xiao." I thought suddenly how I liked saying her name out loud. I had mastered the accent and her name was like poetry, like a soft breeze.

"I will cook a meal that you will like," she said. "American food."

"Wait. Not now. Come with me."

I led her into our tiny bedroom and sat on the bed, pulling her onto my lap. Xiao was startled; I could see it as I brushed the hair from her face. I kissed her and she didn't push me away.

"Put this on me," I said, pushing the necklace into her hand.

"Your shirt is in the way," she said.

I stripped off my shirt and tossed it in a heap on the bed.

Wordlessly, Xiao leaned up against me to manage the tiny clasp.

"Xiao…"

"Almost done."

I put my arms around her.

"There," she said, "done." I didn't let her lean away from me but pulled her closer, against my bare chest. She was breathing in my ear. I could hear my own breathing, too. Good God everyone in the building could hear it.

"Xiao," I said again, my mouth against her cheek. I pulled her off my lap, rolling her onto the bed. Any fear I might have had of crushing her was gone. The jade necklace hung between us as I hovered over her.

"It's beautiful," she whispered.

"You're beautiful," I said.

"Show me."

I began with unbuttoning her chemise, then fluttered my fingers over her neck, her shoulders, her breasts until she lowered my mouth to first one, then the other. I couldn't tell the difference between tasting her sweet skin and smelling its soft perfume.

She said my name. It was permission.

I rolled off her to watch as she slid her skirt over her narrow hips and kicked it away. Then her thong. Then there was Xiao, open, brazen and afraid. We became a tangle of cool skin on skin, frenzied kisses, with her hurried hands between us until I was nearly naked and then I was on top of her again. We were fluid, harmonic, one, as we poured ourselves into one another.

*****

I dozed and when I woke, she was singing in the kitchen.

Good. She was still here.

I ducked into the bathroom, noted my own sated expression. Hmmmm. I splashed my face and looked around for a towel—had she unpacked them already?

And then I noticed the faint outline of footprints on the toilet seat. I grabbed a wad of bath tissue to clean it off. Was there a bathroom ghost here? No. I laughed realizing it had been Xiao, who, afraid of germs and accustomed to the public floor-hole toilet styles, had likely assumed a standing position on the toilet lid that I hadn't learned to appreciate. Washing my hands, I decided I would speak to her about it. But now wasn't the time.

"Xiao," I called.

I started toward the kitchen. Thick black smoke was filling the main room of the apartment. "Xiao!"

She was fanning the smoldering wok and crying. After opening the tiny kitchen window, I uncovered the wok, and inside, blackened in a bath of sesame oil, was the small frozen pizza I'd purchased hours earlier. She fumbled turning off the burner. I wanted to laugh. I wrapped my arms around her instead.

"I need a microwave or an oven," I explained.

"But we don't have those."

"Hey, it's OK. I bought the pizza because it was familiar to me, I was excited. We just can't have it yet." She broke away from me. I picked the remains of the pizza out of the wok and tilted the garbage can open, but Xiao stopped me, grabbed it, sat down on the living room windowsill and began to eat it.

Had it been anyone else, I would have called them stubborn or silly. But this was Xiao, a woman who, the more I knew her, the more I loved her and this country. So familiar, the two, country and woman, exotic landscapes.

I sat down next to her on the windowsill and held out my hand. Silently, she broke off a chunk and passed it to me. I ate, trying not to laugh.

Be patient, I told myself. And it was then that Xiao broke into hiccupping laughter until tears ran down her face.

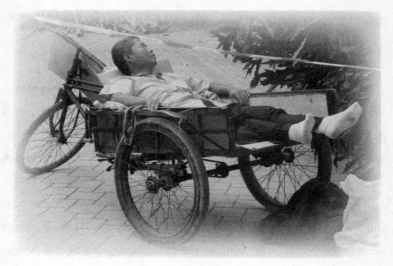

Ten

I had met two other businessmen at a local hotel networking party. One, Francois, was French-Canadian, and the other, Billy, hailed from Missouri. I glommed onto Billy like a long-lost brother.

Over several bottles of beer, we quickly become compadres, independent souls seeking our fortunes in China. Francois was connecting with high-tech firms, mainly wireless Internet router businesses, plus he was into manufacturing copycat products. Billy's expertise was furniture. He built small display samples to show customers who would then place orders. He said his Chinese factories could build hand-crafted table and chair replicas for one-fourth the U.S. cost.

I told him my big ticket deal was in solar-powered toys. Toy trains

80

were hot, and my new concept, an alternative-energy toy train, would be a sure winner. I was going to ride my own little money train, my multi-million dollar money train.

After learning Billy was living in a hotel room (big surprise), I convinced him to rent an apartment in my building, and as luck would have it, he landed on the floor above my own space.

One morning, at eleven, the pounding beat of hammer on wood jolted me out of bed. I had stayed up late the night before, fielding phone calls from the U.S., setting up meetings and conferences concerning my train project, and I was no way ready to face the day. Pulling on my sweats and a gray t-shirt, I marched up the stairwell to Billy's door, and pounded on his door. The hammering stopped and I heard footsteps clomping across the floor.

"Hey you, what's up?" His dust-covered face peeked out the open door.

"Your hammering is what's up. What are you doing?" I said, trying to be pleasant.

"Oh, sorry. Did I wake you? I figured you'd be out the door by now. I'm working on some samples for the factory."

"Samples?" I looked over his shoulder and there were wooden frames and lumber and sawhorses. The smell of cut oak and sawdust mingled with the humid air.

"Yep. I'm working on an Irish harvest table. The top is made of pine, and I'm working on the legs. Probably go with a French-style leg. You know, a little curve."

I had no idea what a "French-style leg" was, but I was amazed by his

81

studio, and felt a tad envious that I didn't have the ability to create such works of art. My skill was working with words, not wood.

"Do you want me to knock it off for a while, Ben? I can. It's no problem." He said, smiling through a layer of sawdust and wiping at his eyes.

"No, that's fine. You keep doing what you're doing. I'm up, anyway."

"You want me to start a little later tomorrow?"

"No, eleven's just fine. I can't wait to see what the final product looks like."

"Me either. But I need to have it done by the weekend. The factory needs to take measurements and get their tooling set up. And I can't get my startup money until this is finished." He looked back at the table and shrugged. "I wish I didn't have to borrow so much, but what am I going to do."

"Which bank are you using?" I asked.

"Bank? No, I'm not going through a bank," he laughed and went back to sanding a display piece. "Have you tried to talk to those guys? It's a million miles of red tape, just to start an account. And they aren't big on lending money to foreigners."

"So—?" I was wondering where this was going.

"Oh, let's just say I have a connection. It's all under the table, secret. The factory owner hooked me up with a money guy here."

The Association! He was taking money from a clan leader. The realization of what he was doing sent a chill up my spine. Dangerous stuff, borrowing from criminals.

"Alright, Billy. You take care of yourself," I held out my hand. "Good luck with the table. Let me know when you're done, I'd like to see the finished product."

"You got it." He said, grabbing my hand. "See you."

He shut the door and as I started down the narrow hallway, I saw someone quickly duck into the elevator.

"Hold it!" I shouted. I wanted a ride, but that shape looked familiar, and I had a good idea who it was.

The doors were closing just as I reached them, but my question was answered. Napoleon's malevolent eyes glared out at me as the doors closed.

Eleven

I sat cross-legged beneath the makeshift clothesline Xiao had fashioned on our balcony and I watched the park across the street. Our jeans and cotton shirts dripped down my back, my bare feet cooled in the puddles of water. The air was unusually sweet, colorless and I felt summer in the air. I closed my eyes and imagined the smells of river water and the deep forests of the Ozark Highlands.

I wondered about China, about its soul, its history, its dragon tenacity. I worried about its people buying products for which they were paid pathetic wages to make. At the knife factory in Yiang-Jiang, Xiao's home town, four hours west of Shenzhen, workers were pulling in $1.50 an hour. Employees lived in dormitories and were given three square

84

meals by their employers. Did it control the labor force? Was it any different in the U.S.? Funny the things you notice when you're a stranger in a strange land. I did know however that no-shows and sick days were not tolerated by employers. But again, was that any different anywhere else? I didn't know but I abhorred the concrete cubicles in which so many lived and went out into the day to work where they squatted on bamboo stools, sharpening kindergarten scissors.

I thought of home and with the vision allowed by time and distance, realized that the American family, too, had its dual-income challenges and time crunches and life quality. Mothers and fathers everywhere were struggling for the sake of their kids, hoping always for a better world. A world that was moving hard and fast despite its stink and contrasting beauty. I was a little worried about the accumulation of "stuff" but then, how was I making a living? On propagating stuff.

*****

My computer beeped and I hurried inside to accept an Internet phone call from Trish.

"How are you?" I asked.

"Good, Ben. Good. I have the jade you asked for. See?" She held a thin red string in front of her webcam.

"Trish, I can't see it." I blinked at the camera, narrowing my eyes to better view the object she was dangling.

She backed her hand away, and the jade pendant came into better focus, a thin, green circle attached to the string. "What do you think,

Ben? Is this what you want?"

"Can you tell me what it means? Does the jade pendant have any special significance?" I wanted her to tell me that it meant Xiao would love me forever, whether I was ready to do the same or not.

"Sure. It means destiny. Your life's meaning. Like fate. Do you want to order some of them? They are very beautiful. And I can get you a good deal," she said.

"Um, no, actually, I don't want to order them. I wanted to know about the circle, what it means. I wondered..."

"Wondered what?" Trish asked, her brow furrowed.

"Is that all, Ben?" she said. Behind her, I could now see her son Andrew, munching on a cookie. Trish would never leave Andrew to anyone else's care. They were the epitome of mother and child, and I secretly envied their relationship. What was it like to be a parent, to have such responsibility?

"Yes. Thanks, Trish. You're a peach." I knew this would get her, in a good way. She could puzzle for a while over being a peach—was it good? Was it bad? "Really, thanks, Trish. I know you're busy at that trade show. In fact, I hope you're super busy—that means business is good. Please give Andrew a hug for me."

I got a smiling "bye bye" out of her before I closed the laptop, and looked at the clock. I had an appointment to keep, and a lot of questions to ask a good friend.

Twelve

Mr. Johnson's office was the penthouse and did not mirror the general aesthetic of the rest of the hotel. Floor-to-ceiling windows circled a large room that contained a sitting area with two leather love seats, one white, one black, separated by a coffee (or was it tea?) table fashioned from a gnarled tree trunk. An exquisite tea set, probably an antique, sat on the table amidst a complex arrangement of implements and ceramics. Tiny white cups were stacked beside a matching teapot. A stainless-steel pitcher and a wooden cup of utensils had been arranged on a hand-carved drip tray.

I would have expected no less from such a meticulous gentleman. Inside his inner sanctum, his office, I felt regal, even chosen.

"Ben! So very good to see you!" Mr. Johnson said, his left hand covering his desk phone's mouthpiece. "Just a minute, and I'll be with you. Please sit." He waved at the small sofas, and I decided to sink into the white love seat.

After several minutes, he joined me. I rose and we shook hands, then gave each other a slight nod.

"Have you had traditional Chinese tea?" he asked. Before, tea was a perfunctory act, in the hotel restaurant, cups, blazing-hot pitcher, and ground black leaves sealed in a traditional, metallic ball. But now I saw a tray made of polished driftwood, delicate, ivory cups, and assorted alien accoutrement.

"Well, I've had tea, but I'm not sure if it was traditional." I eyed the pitcher, cups and accessories on the table, knowing this would be more than just boiling and pouring.

"Oh, you would know," he smiled. "There are many things to show. Here." He pointed to a side table, where several small, ornate canisters sat. "Do you like strong tea, or something more mild?"

"I like strong tea."

"Very good. OK, so."

He opened the canister, then deposited two scoops of dried tea leaves into a metal strainer, which he then placed in the stainless-steel container.

"I must wash the leaves," he explained.

From his hot water tap, he poured steaming water over the leaves, and then dumped the water out, pouring it over the small teapot. The water ran down the sides of it, and was collected in a hidden base under the tea tray. After two more washings, he filled the container again, and this he poured into the tea pot.

He put a tiny cup in front of me, and filled it. We held our cups, and he nodded. I followed and sipped. The tea was rich and floral. If the color green had a flavor, this would be it.

"Do you like it?" he asked.

"I do, very much." I savored the floral flavor as it glided down my throat. It's unfortunate we Americans are too hurried to take the time to enjoy the tea ceremony, I thought. A quick cup of coffee over the newspaper or CNN, then off to work, maybe a drive-through run. Unlike its coffee counterpart, tea told me to slow down, to relax.

"When you would like more tea, you do this," Mr. Johnson said, and tapped his right index and middle fingers on the table.

"Is that how a person asks for a refill?" I asked.

"It is, and do you know why?"

"No idea."

Mr. Johnson put his teacup down, and sat back. "Supposedly it comes from a very ancient emperor. Hundreds of years ago, he came south, from Beijing, and wanted to see how his countrymen lived. He did not want to be noticed, so he dressed like a peasant, as did his security detail."

"And tapping his fingers was a way to signal them, wasn't it?" I was proud of myself for figuring this out.

"You are very smart," Mr. Johnson said, reading my mind. "But the emperor was not signaling his bodyguards. The two knuckles represented a person kneeling, like bowing."

"But they couldn't kneel, right?"

"No, it would give away the emperor's status, and he did not want that. Two knuckles on the table. Kindred spirits sharing a simple gesture of rapport, of relationship. He always knew their location."

"So they signaled him, when he was sitting at a table drinking tea, or playing mah jong, China's version of poker."

"Yes." Mr. Johnson continued, "And the people of Canton adopted this signal when requesting more tea. If you are single, you tap the tips of your fingers. If you are married, you use your knuckles."

"And I guess it still shows reverence, like kneeling or bowing. It's a courtesy, and it takes less time than the American way of saying 'please' and 'thank you,' huh?"

My cup was empty, and while he was pouring the delicate liquid into his cup, I tapped my fingertips to ask for a refill. Mr. Johnson smiled and filled my petite cup.

I noticed the beautiful framed calligraphy around his office, and asked, "What do they mean, what is written there?"

He blushed and said, "That is a fault. I spent probably too much money on them. Very famous Chinese writer made these for me, see?" He pointed to a red character stamp at the painting's lower right edge. This one tells a story about the Autumn Moon Festival, the second most important Chinese holiday. Do you want to know what that is?"

"Very much so," I answered.

He turned to the painting and said, "Many centuries ago, lived a boy known as the 'boy of shadows' for he only crept about the city streets and alleyways after the sun gave up the day, and purple twilight brought the moon.

"The boy loved the moon. In fact, he had given it a special name: 'White Ghost.' Although the boy had no one to care for him, he was never lonely, for his White Ghost was usually near, glowing above him, whether full, half, or splintered into a thin crescent.

"Most of the locals were wary of the full moon, but not the boy. To him, the fullness of the white orb filled him with love and longing. The moon was the face of a beautiful mother who whispered in his ear, telling him of daylight and darkness, of acceptance and rejection, of love and death."

Mr. Johnson paused, bowed his head and kept silent for a moment, allowing his words and their meaning to take root. Then, he continued.

"One particular evening, the Ghost moon told him her deepest truth. She said to the boy, as he reclined on a dirty pile of refuse, that she was, in fact, a great liar. He clutched at the vermillion thread tied about his neck, and the quartz stone engraved with his birth icon, a dragon.

"Why," demanded the boy, "would you call yourself a liar? You are good and decent, and you care about me, I know it. You are not a liar. You are beautiful."

"My pretense is a great mystery, little one," the Ghost moon replied, "The deception is my light."

"How can you say that!" the boy cried. "Your light is sweet and soft. Unlike the Sun, you change yourself; you turn, you whirl, you reduce, you grow. But always your light is gentle and revealing. Your light reveals a place to rest or food to pick from the alley bins. You give me just enough light so that I can see and not be seen. It is because of your wonderful glow that I am able to live and survive in this horrid place.

"It is the Sun I hate, with his constant burn, his frown, his hateful, spitting gaze. He grows harsh in the summer and apathetic in the winter. He is inconsistent. But you, dear Ghost, are constant."

The Ghost told the boy, "And that consistency is the veil which hides the lie, dear one. My light is not real; I am only a reflection of the sun, a wisp of its warmth redeemed in the darkest of night. I am not real. You should not love me so. Look at your dragon-stone."

The boy pulled at his necklace, and it broke, and he realized the quartz was unmarked. Its flat surface, bathed in moonlight, revealed a space as empty as the night itself, the dragon etching had disappeared. In its place, a dog had appeared.

"Under a sheet of stars, the boy fell into a deep sleep and dreamt his usual dreams, about faraway lands, oceans, and the face of the moon, except she wasn't a bleached circle in the dusky sky. She was holding him, and stroking his raven hair, and her mouth only moved to kiss his forehead, and she pulled a lavender blanket of night sky over him, and laid his head in her lap, and sang ancient, beautiful songs."

Touched by the emotion of the story, I sat back and considered his words. "Mr. Johnson, what does the Moon Festival mean, really? Is it some kind of harvest celebration?"

He got up and poured us some more tea, then after handing me my cup, he sat down.

"The story goes like this: the earth represents the boy who loves a girl. She is the moon. She loves him, too, but they can never be together; they are destined to always be apart. The Moon Festival is a reminder of that desire, to love even though you risk never being together. Sometimes it is one's destiny to only have the desire and not the reality of the situation."

"Like Xiao and me."

"Are you together?"

"Yes and no. I have to make a decision about that. Soon."

"So she is your moon, and you are the Earth. It's tragic to be apart, when you are so in love."

"Yes. Tragic," I said, more to myself than my mentor. "Unless something changes, and that is up to me."

"Do you love her?"

"I do."

"Well, then?" He smiled, and patted my back. "You will make a good decision, Ben. You are a good man."

I thanked him and shook his hand. Outside, I hailed a taxi and during the short drive home, stared at the shifting moon as it appeared above the horizon. Xiao would be home, lighting incense on the patio, a delicious pot of seafood stew bubbling on the stove. We would eat, meditate, and watch the moon dominate the black sky. I clutched the jade circle Xiao had given me and thought about my destiny with her.

Thirteen

*T*hen there was the visa application. I was bound and determined to get one for Xiao, so she could sample my culture. We made headway into the process; it was like pounding our heads against a tough bureaucratic wall, but it was headway nonetheless.

We first had to scratch the surface of the complicated morass of government wiring. Apparently only five in 1,000 applications processed were accepted, said the American embassy, and it would cost a small fortune. However, by paying off some regional inside officials, Xiao's chances increased by 50 percent, and I liked that potential a lot more than paying a travel agent for lesser odds. So we traveled to Guangzhou to meet this insider, review our paperwork, and get some solid numbers on payoff antes.

*****

My stomach rumbled. I had been careless about my diet, chowing down on this and that from boutique-type eateries, likely with no business certificates

"Xiao, I gotta take it easy on the off-the-beaten path foods. Listen to me—I'm a digestive orchestra."

She ignored me for a moment, then said, "I feel no emotional anger toward you."

"Huh? What does that mean?"

"You don't listen to me," she said and turned away.

I had been busy with factory meetings. My cell phone, regardless of where we were—in the apartment, out at dinner, playing badminton in the park, was constantly chirping. If my cell rang, I answered. If it didn't ring, I worried and initiated calls.

And now I realized I had not corrected a computer glitch for Xiao, one that would assist her Chinese-English translations. At my behest, she was writing a Cantonese cookbook, and she needed to translate colloquial phrases. But my so-called lack of attention had caused her, and her work to suffer. Damn, she had asked for help days ago and I hadn't said a word, nothing, zip, nada, hadn't even thought of it until now.

"I'm sorry, I'll fix it today."

"No, Ben. Me. I apologize."

"Why?"

"I do not want you to keep your unhappy feelings in."

"What? No, I'm not unhappy. I should have fixed it for you days ago. You should have said something, yeah, I should have remembered, but you should feel free to say something. Communication is important, Xiao. It makes us better. Talking is good, right?" Didn't women like to talk? Weren't they famous for saying "we have to talk"?

"Is this communication thing a problem because I'm Chinese?" She frowned, stared at me, her eyes darkening.

"No, this is a problem in my country, too. Everywhere, probably. People don't talk and then get unhappy. And then it gets too late and they can't fix it. It's normal. Well, I mean it happens. A lot, I think." I opened my arms and she walked into them, snuggling against me. I held her close. I was touched by her, by her drive to please. I mean, I wasn't used to it. Call it submission, call it whatever you like. I felt closer for it.

"Ben, I want you to visit mother." She was talking into my armpit.

"You want what?"

She tipped her face up to mine.

"You want me to go back home to my mother?" I said.

"No, meet my mother here."

"You want me to meet your family?"

"Yes, and your birthday is tomorrow. I have your gift."

"Are you giving me a gift because I agree to meet your family or because it's my birthday?" Sometimes, I didn't understand how she connected things.

"Have it now." She produced a small brown box tied with red string from her sweatshirt pocket.

Inside, under a thin gauzy layer of red tissue were two white-gold rings tied together with pink ribbon. For a split second I panicked, and out loud, I was even more moronic: "Where did you get the money for this, Xiao?" I meant it nicely, I was overwhelmed. My question sounded harsh, rude.

"Mother gave me money to buy jewelry, so I bought two rings." When did she see her mother? Did her family know that Xiao was living with me? Better not be any shotguns coming up, riding down main street, barrels loaded and pointed at me. Nope, didn't want a wedding thing, not yet, not me.

Anyway, I didn't believe her about the money. No big deal. It was a nice gift, too, but I realized she was pushing me, in a not-so-subtle manner, toward commitment. Chinese girls were not so unlike their American counterparts. I was a bit unsettled yet also somehow flattered.

"So we can see my mother tomorrow?" she said.

"Tomorrow? Um, sure. So, which finger do I wear this ring on, I mean, since we're not married...which one?"

"The middle finger is fine." Well, she wasn't going to back down on the ring thing. No sign at all of that sweet submission witnessed moments prior.

So we put our rings on our left middle fingers, and I felt like a high school kid, an adolescent playing with promises and jewelry.

The next day, we loaded our backpacks with simple weekend outfits, bottled water and energy bars. On the way to Yang Jiang, we stared out the bus windows at emerald mountains, at waterfalls that rendered farmland lush, at banana trees, rice paddies, and fisheries. A romantic comedy played on two TV monitors, and the familiar stench of cigarettes emanated from the toilet, which appeared to double as a tiny smoking lounge. The bus attendant continually, and bravely, stuck his head in there to berate the passengers who lit up despite the no smoking signs.

Sometimes I watched Xiao gaze out the window, lost in her own thoughts. Maybe she was worried about bringing a ghost-man home to meet the family matriarch.

*****

Seven hours later we arrived and fell out of the bus into the hazy, fall afternoon. Old motorcycles and bicycle rickshaws wove through the streets, advertising their taxi services. I found a driver in a rusted compact car and off we went while "dinner with the family," my own cartoon version of how the family encounter would go, played over and over in my head:

Ben, this is Mother; Mother this Ben. (Bow, handshake, whatever, but smile, smile, smile.)

"How do you do?" I ask, the informal, imprecise language of my culture. I'm nervous, of course.

"I am well," Xiao's Mother says, "and it is very nice to finally meet you, the boyfriend. Welcome." She spreads her arms like a preacher, and behind her, the family is revealed, and of course they are smiling, bright, white grins. They surround me and shake my hand, and Xiao beams, glad of her family's response, but she's clearly relieved.

There is a massive dining table piled with delicious food and cold glass bottles of cola. We dine and have great conversations (everyone speaks English in this dream), and I am welcomed into the bosom of her family whose curiosity is flattering rather than frightening.

And then her parents notice the white-gold rings on our fingers, and they place their palms on their cheeks and their eyes grow large.

"Are you engaged?!" they exclaim in unison.

"Yes!" Xiao replies.

"No!" I say, louder than I intended.

Xiao gently pushed my arm and I woke.

"We are here," she said. I was sweating in spite of the cool air. We paid the driver, gathered our packs, and climbed out. A corner marketplace was crowded with bins and baskets of fruits and vegetables. Chickens and geese protested from wooden cages. Xiao grabbed my hand, pulling me past a farmer who just beheaded a goose. I imagined bird flu flying up out of its twitching carcass. She pointed to a nearby, three-story concrete structure, and I followed her. We were in the ghetto. I was surprised and disappointed as we entered the building.

On the third floor, Xiao sang out in her Yang Jiang dialect, and a tiny older woman and little girl came quickly into the hall, laughing, bowing, weeping with joy, I thought, but I was wrong. Turns out she was scolding Xiao for something but the little girl, the little spritely thing, came jumping up at Xiao, begging her attentions until she bent and held her little face in her hands and kissed her.

I swore under my breath because I had forgotten my camera. The woman invited me into a cramped apartment and pointed to a wood chair. I sat while Xiao and the other two settled onto plastic stools mere inches from the ground.

Xiao smiled and spoke to her mother, then turned to me saying, "Let's eat!" And out came the food amidst the flurry of the two women and the child who paraded around the table carrying a huge bowl of something that turned out to be a fish stew, with the fish completely intact, their eyeballs rolling out of their heads. There was rice. Shrimp, also with heads intact. Bowls of clear soup, thank God, but each accompanied by a tiny roasted chicken. And, there was a bowl of wet odd vegetables.

I was stunned. I was starving, too but I wasn't going to eat. Not this. My stomach was sending a resounding "no" to my lips. One bite of this stuff and I'd be in the hospital, if there was one.

Sick, I tried to explain. I'd get very sick. This caused a great amount of confusion until Xiao calmed everyone and fixed a plate with rice and the clear soup for me.

The little girl, Mei, fought with a little fellow who had materialized from somewhere in the building though I supposed him to be a brother. Both children wanted the fish eyes. I couldn't imagine what for. Mei's long, dark hair was pulled into a thick ponytail, like Xiao's. Rolling around the apartment on skates, she stopped and twirled, and eyed me suspiciously. The same look Xiao would give when she asked deep questions.

*****

After dinner, we sat and the women talked. Just like home. Except I couldn't understand a word.

When the old woman hid herself into the kitchen, ostensibly to clean up, I turned to Xiao and asked, "Where is the rest of your family, your father and your sister and brother?"

"Out with friends," she said.

"Oh. Where does everyone sleep?"

"My mother and father have a room. Brother and girlfriend have a room, too."

"What about you? Your sister?" I motioned at Mei.

She acted like she didn't understand the question, and gave a mumbled response and turned back to her food. Hmm. I shrugged. I was curious, I was being polite, but more than anything, I was still hungry. How many energy bars were still in my backpack? I glanced over at the corner where it sat. My rat-must-eat thoughts were interrupted by a parade of new faces coming through the door. "Hello" some said in English, giggling, which I swear is a practiced art among Chinese kids.

Xiao said these were neighbors who wanted a look at the white ghost. With all the fawning, giggling, babble of a dialect I did not at all understand, I was soon smiling at Xiao and growling softly at her about leaving.

"We're going," she said, standing and taking me by the hand. "We need to check in to our hotel and clean up."

Right, and that's not all, my gurgling stomach said. Fortunately no one heard it.

*****

Once in our room, I stashed our stuff in the small chest of drawers while Xiao used the bathroom. I stripped and grabbed a fresh towel and was glad for a whiff of its light bleachy scent. We got ready for an evening at the local karaoke bar. We were meeting Xiao's old friends, and bringing along her little sister, Mei.

*****

Later, everyone roared with laughter as one of Xiao's friends stuck a red and white can in my face. Budweiser! They were glad to offer me a familiar beer.

"Thank you," I said, and pointed at a nearby Tsingtao, the only beer I could drink without getting a jackhammer headache. I felt a momentary guilt at declining the King of Beers, but so what? Did it matter on a grand scale? Tsingtao wasn't going to put Anheuser Busch out of business any more than a Chinese 747 would mean the end of Boeing's business back in St Louis. Then again—I put the Tsingtao down, raised the Budweiser, and shouted, "Gum-bai!"

The drinking games began, and Xiao's friends laughed. As the evening wore on, I drank both beers and hoped that I was friendly enough. At the epicenter of the verbal hurricane around me, with the sad, yet curious eyes of little Mei watching my every move, I felt very vulnerable.

The night raged on with more beer games. I was chastised into performing some all-American karaoke. After I wailed out an Eagles tune, little Mei sang a sweet, incomprehensible song. Hours later, we were saying goodbye and carrying the little girl back to our room, her

102

head resting heavily on my shoulder. I had to confess it gave me a warm feeling. Or, it could have been the beer talking.

*****

We faced another day with Xiao's family but this time, took a leisurely stroll through the market, admiring the fruit tended by farmers in filthy clothes with the cleanest smile anyone on this good earth could muster and yet their faces were otherwise expressionless. Like dolls.

Xiao hailed a nearby rickshaw, and I just stood there, looking at the decrepit tricycle. "Not to worry," Xiao said, pulling on my arm, pulling me in to her. A habit of hers lately, I noticed.

"Safe," she said, "Safe and easy."

Fine.

Lunch was a mere ritual, with the women preparing the food, preparing the plates, holding up things I might like, an inquiring expression that said "Try this? No? Try this, then?" Her mother seemed apathetic really about my presence and made no move or effort to discover anything about this white giant in her abode.

We left. Mei came with us to visit more friends and though I suspected this was to show off the white boyfriend, I couldn't say anything.

Mei avoided me, however, though I was the winner of more backward glances than I was stares from the locals. Xiao explained that Mei was afraid of the hair on my face and my white skin. OK, fine, normal for any five-year-old, I thought. For some reason, I felt like an interloper, a short-term father figure, who was coming between a little girl and her mother. Mei's eyes flashed, and I felt her fear. Looking away, I realized how alien I felt at that moment.

I recalled the first time I had seen an African-American woman in a hospital elevator. I had turned to my mother and asked, "Is she burned?" The woman laughed and smiled and my mother apologized, but the woman waved away the explanation and said it was alright.

Now I glanced at Mei and asked what she supposed had happened to make me so light-colored. Xiao translated, and Mei said, "Not much sun!" Her laughter eased the tension between us, and I smiled, too.

After an hour of making the rounds, shaking hands, and being the object of stares, we dropped Mei off at the apartment. The little girl began to protest, so Xiao held her and sang to her. She kissed her sister's forehead, and set her back on the ground, crouched, and had a small conversation while Mei pouted.

We left for the bus by rickshaw. My confidence in the traffic and in myself had grown. I couldn't, however, shake the feeling the last two days had been scripted. I felt like I'd met actors, Chinese mendicants hired to play roles for the white ghost. I held Xiao's hand and we traveled back to Shenzhen, and again she stared out into the void, deep in her own thoughts.

******

A month later, we made the same trip, stayed in the same hotel and endured the same familial visit though we did manage to take everyone out for dinner. Including the brother and his girlfriend, though Dad was still among the missing.

"Shh shhh," Xiao said. "He's very busy. Doing business." Good enough for me. Her sister didn't make an appearance, either, but since Xiao didn't seem to care, neither did I. Mom still hadn't warmed up particularly, but that was OK and I was glad actually that this wasn't a hugging culture. Mom sat on her short stool and chatted away while I sat back in the wood chair and smiled and nodded. East was East and West was West.

That Sunday, the day of our second visit, we hired a taxi for the morning and headed to the beach. It was clean and beautiful, a vast expanse of perfect sand against the ocean's swirling, foamy blue. I lay on the oversized towel, under our umbrella, the beach crowded with noisy families, half naked in the cool air. They stared at us, of course. We didn't care.

A child screamed. I couldn't see her until I jumped to my feet, but I knew immediately that the cries were Mei's. She had been knocked down by a wave and now stood trembling and howling at the shoreline. I ran to her and gathered her up. What was the crowd thinking now of the little girl and the big white ghost? Was she his? Was she a happy accident? I laughed at my imagination, and Mei giggled, too, grabbing at my ears. I set her down and we ran zigzagging across the sand.

*****

That night, Xiao was leaving our room with all our clothes, soiled and rancid, permeated with the sulfur smell of Yiang Jiang.

"What? Where are you going?" I asked, looking up from my laptop.

"I'm taking laundry to my mother." She laughed. There was a habit that just never went away. It was understood and accepted stateside that when you went home, you took your laundry with you for your Mom to do.

"We need clean things for our return to Shenzhen tomorrow. Stay here. Do your work." She pointed to my Internet headphones. "You have calls to make, and I won't be gone long."

I nodded and got back to work, sorry in some small way that we had to go back "to town" tomorrow. Two hours later, as night fell, Xiao showed up carrying an armload of freshly folded laundry.

"Hurry, change!" she commanded, "We are going to a friend's party!"

I dressed quickly and was immediately aware of a woodsmoke smell. "What the...?" I lifted my shirt and pressed it to my nose. Smoke? I smelled like a fireplace.

"OK, come clean, Xiao. Did the laundry take two hours because you were drying it over a fire?" She looked away, ashamed.

"I'm sorry, Ben. We didn't know what to do. There was no time to air dry your clothes."

"Xiao, look at me." She turned and looked at me over her shoulder. "I love what you did. Thank you."

Yeah, that was me talking, Mr. Wheeler Dealer, Mr. Make it Right, Mr. Some Small Modicum of Success, finally learning to talk nice. And mean it.

It was worth the ridiculous bus trip to see Xiao with Mei although their tearful goodbyes at the end of the weekend were on the gut-wrenching side, that is, if you cared about either of them. And I certainly did.

Fourteen

Three o'clock in the morning, and I was sweating profusely. I wasn't dreaming, I had literally pinched myself to make sure. I put my feet on the floor, and felt the cold tile and the chill in the air. I listened again for what woke me—the sound of a woman's heels clicking on our floor.

Xiao was standing at the window, or I thought it was Xiao, dressed in a blur of red and gold. I felt a strange sense of déjà vu. I looked to my right, but there was Xiao lying snug in bed. So who was at the window?

I whirled around. The distorted Xiao-phantom was looking at me with a confused expression in her eyes. In an instant, she turned to the open window and vanished between the metal blinds; they rattled like iron wind chimes, and I rubbed my eyes and called out to her. "Wait!

Come back! What do you want?"

I turned back to Xiao. Her eyes darted behind her delicate eyelids. She was dreaming, deep in a heavy ocean of sleep, even through my loud calls.

Her cell phone vibrated, skittering on the nightstand. I jumped out of my reverie, grabbed it, and nudged her. She opened her eyes, took the phone, and spoke in dialect. I knew it was family business. My Mandarin was improving, and I translated several words: mother, sister, night, dead.

After five minutes, she gently closed the phone and tucked it under her pillow.

"My mother," she answered my unspoken question.

"Why did she call?"

"Cannot sleep. Felt spirit. Spirit of her daughter. She woke up. Said for a moment she thought it was me standing next to her bed."

She said she had told her mother to go back to sleep, that she was just nervous about the upcoming New Year celebrations. "Year of the Dog," she said. "Good luck year. Everyone is nervous, planning parties."

Chills ran up my spine. This apparition had been at our window at the same time it had been at Xiao's mother's. This all had to mean something, but what?

I paced around the room and touched the jade circle tied about my neck. I began to imagine every bit of bad luck centered there, the mafia scare, the commitment worries, the ghost who haunted my mind. And she was real, wasn't she? The ghost was real. Hey pal, maybe it's time to check into a sleep clinic. You're starting to believe in the supernatural.

You're starting to become one of them. Black cats, bad omens, and the fear of the number four. What's next? Oh yeah, I was seeing ghosts.

*****

Hours after Xiao had drifted back to sleep, I crawled into bed beside her, and pulled her to me. She stirred, whispered my name, and I just lay there, holding her, waiting for blessed sleep which did not come. The pendant, I thought. Get rid of it. Get rid of the bad luck that's been hounding me. I slipped out of bed, yanked the pendant from my neck and threw it in the trash. There, I thought. It will go from trash to landfill, back to the earth where it belongs. I changed my mind, though, and fished it from the waste bin, and put it back around my neck. A gift from Xiao wouldn't bring bad luck, I told myself.

Crawling back into bed, I finally dozed off. I dreamt about a cigar box filled with a little boy's treasures, and underneath the detritus of youth, under the bits of Lego blocks, green army men, and matchbox cars, a tiny golden dog was buried. And then, I was the boy again, digging with a shovel, digging for the buried canine, but the shovel wouldn't bite through the soil, which was now a sludge of wet baseball cards and rubber superballs.

I heard the dog bark, and then the voice of my father, his gentle hand resting on my shoulder and he drew close, as October blew in from the North. A purple swatch of night, cold icing the air, and my dad told me that it was OK, that Sam had been a very good dog, and that he had gone

110

to dog heaven and was playing fetch and eating doggy treats and having his tummy rubbed. He said I could let him go, and then, in my hands, the jade circle appeared.

"What does it mean?" I asked my father. I turned to him, but he was gone.

"It is your destiny," the ghost whispered into my ear, the jade circle bright and liquid in the moonlight.

*****

Shenhzen's incessant construction had become my alarm clock. Jackhammers bit into asphalt, electric concrete saws divided wall studs, and welding torches glazed metal trusses.

Xiao wrapped her arms around me and kissed my cheek.

"Buy a bed," she said without warning.

"What?" This was not what I perceived to be lovers' morning conversation.

"Buy a bed," she repeated. "I want to buy a new bed."

I realized, then, I had told her we needed a new mattress, something to sleep on, not the thin foam slice upon which I tossed and turned. It was like sleeping on a box spring. After a quick breakfast of melon and toast, Al arrived and drove me to Wal-Mart. Or Wall-R-Mart. Whatever. I hoped that this was not going to become a habit.

We walked down the rows of mattresses. I had not the foggiest idea on how to pick the best one, and Al was no help. About six salespeople flocked after us, chattering, trying to help. Each time we stopped, they stacked up like ten pins behind us. I began to pat and pinch various samples. We sat and bounced on a few.

"Why don't you lay down?" Al suggested. "I've seen people do that."

"Good idea," I said, so I stretched out on one while the salespeople hovered over me like vultures circling roadkill.

Maybe it was the overzealous salespeople; maybe this one felt good. I don't know, but I knew I had to get out of there, so I just picked the most expensive mattress, figuring it would be the softest one, and made arrangements to have it delivered.

*****

Hours later, as I was sitting in a factory board room, trying to drum up support for Al's and my project, my cell phone vibrated. It was Xiao. I turned my head from the assembled company officers and whispered that I was in an important meeting.

"The mattress is here!" I could tell how she excited she was.

"OK, and how do you like it?" I shuffled out of the room and stepped into a hallway. "Do you like it?" I repeated.

"I don't know. I'll have to sleep on it."

"You sound weird. Is everything alright?"

"We have a party tonight."

"You mean the Moon Goddess festival? Sure. I can't wait. Do you want Pizza Hut?" I figured dropping the name of her favorite Western food would elicit some warmth.

"No, we have to see fireworks, and meet my grandmother."

"Really?" This was a surprise. "I'm going to meet your grandmother?"

"Yes. Do you want to?"

"I do," I reassured her, wondering at the suddenness of the meeting. "Let me finish up here, and I'll be home soon. So, do you like the new mattress?"

"I said I don't know. I'll tell you tomorrow." Good answer, I thought. I had heard the Chinese tended to prefer harder beds, and needed time to acclimate to the softer Western mattresses. Guess I would find out.

*****

Xiao, evidently, liked surprises. I was tired, and ready to shower and have a Tsingtao and relax before our big evening, but we had company. Xiao's brother, Yung, had arrived with Mei in tow. The little one ran to me and grabbed my leg, yelping "Be-en!" Xiao quickly collected her small charge. Mei turned and pointed to her and said, "Mal-ma."

Stunned, I looked down at Mei. I said, "Mei, did you just say momma?" She opened her mouth, but Xiao quickly turned her around and kissed her, tossing her gently into the air.

I touched Yung's shoulder and said, "What did that mean, that word, 'Mal-ma'?" He looked at Xiao, and shrugged.

Crammed into the sidewalks, we held hands and walked to our favorite park, which was now crowded with throngs of families. The

113

constant snap of firecrackers sapped the air of its oxygen. We found a place to sit and eat moon cakes while we watched the moon climb higher in the sky. The scent of burning incense permeated the thick air, and I found myself getting caught up in the tradition of it all.

So far, I had not met the grandmother, and wondered when this was going to happen. "Where's your grandmother?" I asked.

She pointed into the purple envelope of space, and said, "There."

"Your grandmother is not the moon," I said, wondering where this was going. "I thought I was going to meet your mother's mom."

"She is everybody's grandmother. The moon is. We celebrate her tonight. She watches over us, she sings songs, she is like the sun, but quiet, not so loud and hot."

I held her hand and shook my head. Superstitions and science were a difficult drink to swallow, but I enjoyed the idea of the Moon Grandmother, and I looked up into the whiteness and said, "Thank you."

*****

Later, I realized man does not live by moon cakes alone, so we walked to Pizza Hut. Xiao and I laughed at Mei who was beyond excited. Yung did not have a lot to say, but seemed to enjoy the pizza and thanked me.

After the meal, we stepped back into the black velvet night.

Mei grabbed my hand and tugged. Perched on my shoulders, she pointed to the moon and said, "Mal-ma." Xiao playfully spanked her rear, and said, "The moon is not your mama." Mei giggled, and looked sideways at Xiao, who quickly picked up her pace and pulled me along.

"We need to go," she said, "we need to light the candle and burn incense. For good luck."

My cell phone chirped, and instinctively, I answered. "Hello?"

"Ben Stillwater," a familiar Napoleon hissed. I stabbed the power button and shoved the phone deep in my pocket. Good luck? I was going to need more than that to deal with Napoleon.

Fifteen

"Are you still seeing the ghost, Ben?" Mr. Johnson asked. We were sitting in his penthouse office, having afternoon tea.

I stopped fiddling with the hourglass on his desk and looked at him.

"Yes, but nothing worth discussing." I paused. "OK, yeah, often. I hear her high heels clicking on the floor and see her, at least I think I'm seeing her, near the window of our apartment.

"Have you approached her?"

"What do you mean?"

"Do you get out of bed and walk to the window? Do you talk with her?"

I wasn't sure why Mr. Johnson was giving my ghost the time of day but the hairs on my arms were standing up.

"The truth is, I avoid looking at her face. I don't want to admit she's there. I don't want to identify her. I am not a ghost whisperer. It's unsettling."

"Does Xiao see the ghost?"

"I don't know."

"Maybe you should ask."

"Yeah? Why?" I was feeling a little testy with his line of questioning. No reason to give this ghost thing more credence than it deserved. Time to change the subject.

"Mr. Johnson, what is your real name—it's not really Johnson, is it?"

"It is Xie Xiao Guang." The words sounded like shu-shou-gwong. "I was born in the early morning. Guang means 'daybreak.' Xie means 'thanks' and Xiao means 'little.' So my name literally means to give thanks as the smallest bit of daybreak begins. My mother said I was a great hope for her. My name also means the line between yin and yang."

"The line between? Interesting." I picked up the hourglass again, thinking. "I've never noticed that line. I just see black and white," I said.

"That is what most people see, the dark and the light. White is heaven, and the dark represents the earth. There must be balance between all things, Ben. The line between the dark and the light is that balance. That is why my mother had hope for me, that I would live my life with balance. And your name, Ben, means what?"

"Son. Favorite son."

"And are you?

"What, the favorite son? Yeah, I guess."

But I was still thinking about the line between the yin and yang. Lucky me. I had a ghost as my line between darkness and light, reality, and fiction. I wondered if a favorite son could also be the spiritual balance in another person's life. I thought of Xiao.

Sixteen

$\mathcal{M}$idnight, and through a semi-conscious state, I heard the staccato popping of heels on the cement floor. Having soaked my bed in night sweat, I unwound my legs from the tight sheets. I followed the sound to my small living area. I had left a window open, and the sheers were billowing out into the night. I gathered them back and closed the window.

Stomach acid burned my throat and I went to the bathroom and brushed my teeth. I stared at my face, and noticed the dark circles under my eyes. Pulling in a short breath, I felt pressure in my chest. Home, I thought, I need to get home. I need fresh air, real sleep, and a good steak.

The next day, my stomach was a tangle of pain and nervous energy. I was unable to eat, and even drinking a bit of bottled water hurt. I prayed to get through the day, through the meetings and conference calls. That night, my sickness manifested itself in the bathroom, and I knew I needed something, anything.

Xiao was spending the day with her family, so I called Al in the morning, and he suggested a corner doctor, only a block from my apartment. I rinsed my face, put on fresh clothes, and walked down the street to find the physician. My bones hurt as I stilted down the crowded walk, and under the haze of factory fog, I saw the neon sign Al had described.

The receptionist did not look up at me until I stood in front of her desk, and then, with a bored expression, asked me what was wrong. Hearing the short version of my complaint, she ushered me into the doctor's office. A lone window opened onto the streets and the smells of food vendors and exhaust wafted in, making me even sicker.

The doctor sat at his desk, poring over a large red book. He looked up at me and asked what was wrong. With my laptop, I translated my condition. He peered at the screen and harrumphed.

"Gui-lao, my family has been in medicine for five hundred years. Don't resist. Take an IV in your arm for four hours," he said.

I noticed then at the far end of the room were about a dozen customers, each sitting like zombies, with clear plastic bags hanging from nearby hooks, needles in their arms.

I replied that an IV drip was the last thing I wanted, or would do. He frowned at my refusal, and scratched a note on paper and handed it to his assistant.

She returned with little glass vials which she handed to the old man. He said it was the next best thing to the IV.

"Just take it," he said, "break glass, vial, and drink. Then take these drugs." He handed me a small bottle filled with tiny black balls. I paid, then walked slowly, wincing all the way, back to my apartment.

I swallowed one of the pills and thought of the chimney at my parent's home, the smell of thick creosote. I felt better within an hour, so I took two more, and floated in and out of dreams. I dreamt of Xiao, but she had blue skin and her mouth was frozen. Her eyes were sad, so I turned her chin in my hand and drew to kiss her, but she fell away from me, and I couldn't find her.

Hours later, when I reached a lucid state, I called Xiao.

"I'm sick," I said. "I won't get any better here, so I'm going home, to Missouri, for a while. To heal." I knew that she wouldn't accept this, and tell me Chinese medicine was better than Western medicine. I was right.

"This is your home," she said, "Take the medicine here."

I trusted my family doctor over a corner herbalist here, but instead of fighting that battle, I explained that I had business in the U.S. anyway, and that I missed my family, not to mention the need to cycle clean air through my lungs. But she wouldn't have it; she even relayed the gossip from her friends in Yiang Jiang. The American boyfriend might have a wife back home.

"I don't believe it, though," Xiao muttered.

*****

I fell asleep as the moon began to peek over the mountains, and dreamt of my mother. I was twelve again, and she was calling up the stairs, waking me for breakfast. I rushed down the stairs, the intoxicating smell of salt pork and butter and strong coffee pulling at me. Amber morning sun flooded the kitchen, and I could hear Mom's voice, but couldn't see her. My eyes adjusted, and she was at the stove, scrambling eggs, her favorite red apron tied about her waist.

"Hurry Ben, pour some milk and eat your breakfast," she commanded. I had to be at school soon, and she had classes to teach. "And let your dog out."

A yellow dog rustled under the table and whined. I reached down, picked up the tiny animal, and brought it to my chest. Somehow I knew this little canine was my dead dog, Sam, a spiritual reincarnation of sorts.

I walked to the back door, and ran through the woods behind our house. Others joined me, childhood friends carrying small objects under their arms, and the finish line was a red rope in the distance, the border of our neighbor's land. I was in the lead, but began to falter, and slowed, afraid I would drop the precious, golden dog in my arms.

I awoke to the familiar sound of Billy's hammering. Eleven o'clock. I smiled and wondered if his table was finished.

Seventeen

*T*he morning air was full of fog and at this height, sixteen stories up, I guess it qualified as a cloud. It was nearly Christmas, and I was playing holiday songs on my laptop, reflecting on what my family might be doing back home and wondering what the middle Missouri countryside looked like. I imagined it like a Kincade painting, all white-blanketed with warm lights shining through every home and storefront up and down Main Street. I thought about the lazy pillar of pinewood smoke above the cabin where I'd spent so many days and nights, the holiday trees still standing in the woods, and the malls decked out like gorgeous garish come-ons.

Here in China, we could hear the Christmas songs and sounds as they wafted up from the streets.

What was going on down there? I asked Xiao who was clattering the dishes back into the cupboard just above her head. "It is almost holiday!" she answered.

"What? The New Year holiday? I thought Chinese did not celebrate the Western holiday. Chinese New Year is twenty-nine days away!"

"No, Ben, they are not celebrating Chinese New Year. Not yet. They are just taking the day off. Shopping."

That afternoon, we pushed through crowds of people, past busy shops where customers were snapping up everything from diamonds to the newest "cool" cell phones—all to celebrate their upcoming New Year. We wanted to be in on the madness but we wanted just as much to find a quiet little corner where we could eat, drink and simply watch the shopping frenzy. I was reminded of Black Friday, the day after Thanksgiving, when American holiday shoppers camped out at stores, then crowded aisles to snatch up the "hot" holiday item.

"So all this activity and...noise... happens every year?"

"Yes. Of course. Remember, too, that many people are off work today. It's Sunday."

"They do this on the actual Chinese New Year, too? The shopping and eating and...swarming?"

"No, on that day, they stay home with family. Ben, you've been here for some time. You haven't seen this before?"

"Actually, no," I said. "I made it a point to be back in Missouri during the holidays. Never seen this." I smiled and shook my head at the enormous micro-economy around us. Buying. Selling. Chinese capitalism, under communist rule. Who would ever have thought this possible?

We moved from the street up onto the sidewalk and suddenly the old familiar smell of fast food turned my head. Had to be McDonald's. Yes, and there it was but unfortunately, there were three customer lines wound out the door and halfway down the block. My stomach growled and didn't want to wait.

"Maybe I could pay someone near the front of the line to get me just a little something," I said, looking desperately at the people who were waiting.

"I'll get in line, Ben." Xiao said, then stopped abruptly, her eyes startled and frozen, looking over my shoulder.

"No, that's OK, Xiao, really I can wait—"

Xiao grabbed my hand and headed us in the direction of the apartment. "Enough," she said. She kept looking over her shoulder, then leaned in to whisper that we were being followed. "No, don't look back," she said as I started to turn around.

"What's wrong? I don't understand—"

"Him," Xiao said flatly, pushing me toward a taxi. My throat clenched, and together, we dove into the small car, and Xiao yelled to the driver. The taxi bolted from the curb like a scared rabbit. Looking out the back window, I saw him, Napoleon, with his trademark black-and-white hats, lunging through the crowd. Something small and black in his hand. Was it the rod again? Or a gun? Either way, I figured he wanted to hurt me. Or us.

*****

"Here, eat this, it will make you feel better," she said, setting hard-boiled eggs and mango juice on our tiny kitchen table. "First, on this day, you have to be careful. A lot of poor people are on the street today, looking for money, however they can get it. They will use it to get back to see family for Chinese New Year. Muggings and petty theft peak on this day. And it's not good to have your white face out there. Too much attention."

"Don't you mean it's not good to be out there when Napoleon's around, looking for us?" I said. My rhetorical question sat between us, until Xiao walked over and put her arms around my shoulders.

"You are OK, Ben?" Xiao whispered into my ear. "I think he is intimidating us."

"Damn right he's intimidating. What does he want? Is he still working for the Association or is it something else he wants? And why in the hell is he trying to intimidate us? He already proved what a laugh riot he can be, with an iron rod in his hand." Xiao missed my sarcasm.

"I don't know. Maybe I should call Clint."

"What's he going to do?" I was irritated.

"Maybe he can help."

I drank the juice, said nothing, pulled at my left ear. It didn't feel right. I didn't feel right. It was one of my favorite holidays, the Christmas into New Year thing and I wanted to join the celebration on the street since I obviously couldn't have my Mom's holiday home cooking and my Dad's fireplace stoked to a roar with wood from our property. That, and I was being followed by a Chinese gangster. My gangster. I laughed at that thought, and then flinched when I swallowed the mango juice.

Oh, I felt like shit. Now my throat was achy. My stomach was quiet, happy with the eggs and juice but I suspected this wouldn't last long. Maybe it was the local pollution, maybe a flu, maybe it was time to go home to the U.S. And then I said it out loud.

"I have to go back home. I need fresh air. I need snow."

"I do not want you to leave, how can you go? Chinese New Year is almost here and I want you with me, with the family."

I shook my head. Dizzy. "No, I need good food. Fresh air. My clothes stink, the air stinks, I need to recharge. My mind is a mess."

"I don't understand."

"No, you wouldn't. That's OK."

Xiao frowned and looked away. She was hurt. I was sorry. But I was hurting, too.

"Get your shoes on, Ben."

"Where are we going?"

"I am going to help you recharge, Ben," Xiao said. "We are going to see someone. Get away, take a vacation." She was going to get me some help. Xiao could take care of things.

As we left the building, she put her arm around me as though to hold me up. I dismissed any thoughts of going back to the States. My pain, and my fear, were temporarily assuaged.

Eighteen

"My Auntie. You need to see her."

"Why?"

"She has the right medicine. She can make you well."

Xiao spoke to the driver, and he nodded and turned the car. We picked up speed, and I asked her how far away. She folded her hands and shook her head. I reclined and closed my eyes.

We arrived at a ramshackle house, with metal nailed over wood and a heavy curtain serving as the hovel's portal.

We walked up a short dirt path, and Xiao knocked on the door. I heard shuffling inside, then a gnarled hand pulled the curtain aside. A little old lady, stooped and withered, looked with rheumy eyes at Xiao, then smiled, showing very few teeth. They hugged, and Xiao pulled me

127

inside.

She explained my medical plight to her aunt, and I understood nothing of what they were speaking. I just hoped she didn't go to the kitchen and start cooking something. I knew something of these home remedies and their ingredients—stuff we wouldn't even use for fish bait in Missouri.

She fixed her eyes on me, then cocked her head to one side and nodded. She opened an old chest on the floor, drew something out and turned toward me.

"You take," she said in a voice so weak, I had to bend to hear.

I looked at her outstretched hand that held a thin ribbon of red, with an engraved quartz stone tied through its gold loop.

"Dragon," Auntie said. "Dragon. You are Dog. Year of Dog is opposite of Dragon. Makes good luck. You wear it. Understand? It is for balance."

"I understand."

"To bring good luck, you must wear it."

I looked at Xiao, and she smiled. I knew she hoped I would not leave, that I would not need the clean air of Missouri, but I didn't believe in hocus-pocus cures. Superstition wasn't going to heal my body.

*****

Later, sitting in the restaurant, I fingered the totem tied about my neck. It rattled against the jade circle. A dragon? Really, was this necessary?

And I knew that it was necessary. It was programmed into the culture, the superstition, the fear of number four (even modern skyscrapers weren't immune—there were no fourth floors), fear of bad omens, colors, people, fear, fear, fear. See that cat? Yep, it's black. And guess what? It's not going to bring bad luck; you will bring your own bad luck!

But I hid behind the laminated menu, and scanned the pictures of Meat Lover's, Deluxe, and the new Hot Wing Pizza! Yuck.

"Xiao?"

She looked at me.

"What are we ordering?"

She shrugged.

"OK. How about the Deluxe, deep-dish sausage, and a pitcher of Diet Coke?"

"That's fine. Oh. And wings," she added. "I want hot wings."

We placed our order, and I traced the red-and-white checkers of the tablecloth. She stared at me until I said "What?" and then she turned away. I fumbled with the dragon again, the totem, my opposite animal, my balance.

It was then I realized "Silent Night" had played a dozen times over the restaurant loudspeakers. I wanted to jump onto the laminate tabletop, grab the nearest speakers, and yank the damn things from the wall. Instead, I called over the manager on duty and Xiao translated my desire for different music. After five minutes of techno-Christmas, "Silent Night" found its way back into the queue. I wondered if this was some hellish, pedagogical method to Westernize employees, to teach them alien holiday music.

*****

Surprise! I told myself, it doesn't feel like Christmas. It was a hazy warm winter day in Bao'an Shenzhen. I tried to think what Xiao and I could do today to make it feel more like the Western holiday of Santa and Jesus.

First, we decided to clean the apartment, then I used the laptop to call home and say my Merry Christmases, fourteen hours ahead of their Christmas Day.

Walking out of the apartment building, we weren't watching where we were going and we literally ran into a couple walking down the street. When I started to apologize, I saw it was a Westerner. Wow, I thought, first Billy, now this guy!

He was a big man by any standards, at least six-feet-seven, and his wide body nearly eclipsed the entire five-foot-zero of his petite wife, with her long dark hair framing a beautiful Asian face.

He was as surprised and pleased to see me as I was to see him. We shook hands and introduced ourselves.

"I'm Colin, and this is my wife, Pei," he said, "We're newlyweds."

He explained that they had had to wait about four to five months for this process and he just recently arrived, he said, to bring her home to Canada. During two years of emailing, he had only met her in person once, ten months earlier.

So, I thought, this is a mail-order bride. I was happy to hear his "happy-ending" story and to meet a Western face. I asked them to join us for Christmas day but they already had plans.

130

"But let's have dinner tomorrow, OK?" he asked.

"OK!" Xiao replied before I had a chance. "How about pizza?"

After exchanging a time and place, Xiao and I headed down town to a five-star hotel reputed to have very good Western food and, with luck, Christmas decorations and a Christmas lunch. Only the higher-end hotels seemed to cater to Westerners. As we arrived I realized my dream. A beautiful Christmas tree decorated in blue and red lights stood outside the hotel. Inside, garland, twinkling lights and colored globes adorned the walls. The buffet offered cheeses, real Italian pasta, salads, vegetables, and carved ham. The aroma of the smoked ham took me back to my home and my mother's Christmas Day dinners.

I piled my plate high with all the food that brought Christmas memories, and we sat down to eat the feast of my dreams. I was hoping that Xiao would enjoy this buffet as there were many dishes that she had never before tasted. I loaded her plate with as many varieties as I could for her to sample so she could savor more of the "Western world" cuisine.

She liked most of the dishes and the smoked ham especially. She had never had this type of pork, so at first, she took a small bite, then when she started to chew and swallow, her eyes lit up. She wanted more. She added another favorite to her list of American food. I paid for our meal and Xiao flagged a taxi.

Under the early afternoon sun, we took a cab to another popular Western hangout, Shekou, about 40 minutes away. As we approached, although I could feel more Christmas spirit, there were not many

Westerners to be found. We met one group of European guys hanging out at a pub and drinking and yelling their seasonal greetings at me. I thought I would ask them if they have seen many Westerners.

"Just you," they said.

I wished them Happy Holidays, grabbed Xiao's hand and took off down the walkway to explore an area that she never knew existed. Christmas lights adorned modest storefronts and trees made from recycled plastic bottles. Some of the Chinese actually dressed up in Santa outfits.

The pedestrian market was packed with Chinese from all classes of poor to wealthy and one gui-lao—me. We decided to walk down to the ocean shore in hopes of getting away from the masses of people. That was not to be. Each street we turned down was lined with vendors and crowds determined to patronize each and every one. Elbows gouged our ribs, other feet trampled on ours, but we persisted to see where all the people were going. Heartbeat racing, I realized I was scanning the crowd for black-and-white ballcaps. I shook off the fear, focused on the holiday spirit and Xiao.

We kept walking and pushing until we saw a big opening where kids were playing and people were sitting around enjoying the late afternoon sun. There were also beggars wandering around, holding up their tin pots in hopes that some generous strangers would drop in a few coins.

In my good Christmas cheer I thought I would give a few of them that were close to me several RMB. That, I soon realized, was a big mistake. As soon as I dropped a few in the nearest container, every beggar within hearing distance charged us, and started pushing and begging with their rusty tin cans.

Panicked by their aggressiveness, Xiao started to scream as we tried to push our way out of the swarm of indigents sticking their cans in our faces. Seeing the commotion, several policemen ran over and escorted us away from the bedraggled bunch.

Xiao smiled and thanked them—at least that's what I assumed she was doing. It was obvious she was relieved to be saved. I offered my hand as a thank you, and we returned to the street of Western restaurants.

A corner Starbucks beckoned, and we went inside to calm our nerves with some caffeine. Go figure, only someone from the Ritalin world of America would need a stimulant to calm down.

"We weren't in any real danger," I assured her. "But it was a little scary, I'll admit."

Xiao nodded, looking up at the menu. Then she slipped her arm through mine and rested her head on my shoulder.

"Two grande mochas," I told the barista.

We sat on a sofa, read some papers and I vowed to be more careful before spreading Christmas cheer the next time.

*****

The next day, we played badminton with our new friends, Colin and Pei. That evening we ate at Pizza Hut and Colin and I shared stories of our China girl dating experiences, how people stared at us with curiosity, yet looked at us like we were Hollywood stars.

Xiao and Pei retired to the ladies' room. Colin said, "What? You look like you want to ask me something." He smirked, and I relayed my fear: marrying Xiao and having to have a big wedding with all her family with whom I cannot communicate.

"I want a small wedding," I said, "if we ever get to that point in our relationship." However, I didn't know what she wanted. I looked over my shoulder, but Xiao was still in the restroom.

"Do Chinese girls dream of fairytale weddings like so many Americans?" I asked Colin. "A Taiwanese friend told me to be careful and lay down the foundation of what I want now or she will have her whole family move in after we get married."

He smiled and nodded. "That's why we're moving to Canada." Colin went on to say how easy it was to get married here in China. They went to the government center, signed a paper and they were married.

"I had to ask her many times if we were married," he said. "I would say, 'Are you sure we're married?' I was surprised that it had been that easy getting hitched in China."

I never thought it would be that simple, and the process, like most things for foreigners in China, seemed very confusing and difficult. Learning the language had been hard enough, and I was glad to find marriage was a relatively simple exercise in paperwork.

If I married Xiao, I thought, I just needed to show proof that we have not made the marriage an "arranged" marriage to get her out of the country, and show proof that we have dated for more than two months— living together was a plus. And there it was, a thought I'd stuffed into the basement of my mind. Marriage to Xiao. That box was now off the shelf, opened, and I couldn't mentally suppress it.

Colin said, "If you're trying to get her citizenship as your new wife, I'm not so sure about how the U.S. works. Canada was easy."

"But," I said, "Canada is probably less restrictive than my country."

"No," Colin replied, "Pei was told she was a very cute, young, single Chinese woman, and getting a visa for Canada could be difficult."

"That's what Xiao said she'd been told," I said. "That the U.S. doesn't like to allow single women in. America is afraid they'll go there just to get married. To get citizenship. She said we had to get married here in China, first."

"Is there something you want to ask me, Ben? Do you want to get married?" Xiao's delicate hands slid from behind my shoulders and she hugged me. She kissed my ear and said, "Well?"

"No!" I yelped, a little too loudly. "I mean, I don't know. I was just, you know, asking Colin some questions." I coughed and lowered my head. Her hands quickly detached and Xiao's expression cooled.

As we ate our dinner, I tried to hold her hand, but she wouldn't have it.

And then Colin and Pei were going to Hainan, China, a paradise much like Hawaii, and they invited us to go along. Xiao became excited, and I agreed, although I hadn't budgeted for a spontaneous vacation. But I also knew that vacations can reveal the strengths and flaws in a relationship. Perhaps our complementary natures would bond, while fissures and indecisions between us might become mammoth divides. We hadn't gone on a vacation—maybe it would force us to examine our future together.

*****

The Hainan beach was a seeping pad of staccato rain and placid ocean.

"I do not feel your love." Xiao walked around the hotel room. I didn't know what was wrong, but this vacation did not have a hopeful beginning.

"Open up your heart and maybe you will feel my love," I said, walking up behind her, and sliding my hands up her smooth shoulders. "Why don't we go have breakfast?"

She jerked away and said she'd lost her appetite.

"Look, what I said at dinner the other night, you know I didn't mean anything. I was only asking questions. I was nervous."

"Do I make you nervous, Ben?"

"How about we take a walk?" I suggested.

We left the beachfront hotel, and I reached for her hand. It was limp and she wouldn't look at me. Our sandals plodded on the sand with the dutiful rhythm of arrogance and pride. Across the expanse of beach, waves drummed the brown grit under our soles and claimed a few bits of quartz.

We came to a dock where an old sailor had roped his skiff to the pier. A single line of crimson paint clung lifelessly to the vessel's bow. He clutched a dingy red cooler and fishing implements. Returning his gracious bow, I waved, and said hello. Xiao looked at me, then translated my greeting. The old man smiled and replied in a different dialect.

"What did he say?" I looked at her eyes.

"He said 'good morning,' that's all." She wouldn't look at me, and instead stared out into the vast horizon.

"Ask him how long he has fished the ocean here."

She conversed with the sailor, the rich sound of Mandarin like a citrusy wine cutting through the seashore fog. "He said since he was a child he fished here. Many years."

"How long do you stay out on the water?"

"He said as long as it takes," she told me.

"How long this time?"

"Four days," Xiao translated.

"Aren't you afraid to be out on the water for that long? To be away from your family?"

"He says to achieve your destiny, you cannot be afraid of time."

I reached for the jade circle and dragon totems around my neck. My hand clasped Xiao's, and I felt the slightest pulse, a squeeze, and she quickly peered into my eyes and then said she wanted to go back to the hotel. She said she was hungry now.

*****

After a small meal of fruit and yogurt, we sat on the sand, while the waves rolled into the sea and pulled at our feet. She watched the foreigners' bodies, and said they look different. Nearly naked, Russian vacationers cavorted and danced into the shimmering ocean. The fleshy, developed breasts, broad bellies, legs, facial features she studied, trancelike. She stared at our new friends, Colin, the Canadian, and his Chinese bride, Pei.

She poked at me when the couple touched and kissed and held hands. I patted the back of her delicate hand, and tried to kiss her cheek, and she pulled away. She turned to her female counterpart and whispered, and they stood and dusted the brown sand from their skinny legs.

When the women went in search of cool drinks, Colin and I talked about the acclimation of habit. Our girls both owned our beds, literally, and pushed us to the edge every night, until we found ourselves hanging on the side. Dominating our diets with talk of can and cannot eat this or that. Some foods good in winter. Some foods better to eat in summer. Soups for the heart, liver, soul.

Colin said, "Do not talk to another girl."

"Oh, yeah, I've heard that sentence come out of Xiao's mouth more than once."

Colin shook his index finger at me, and in a high-pitched voice said, "Do not reach to help another girl, that is not done." I grinned, and he continued, "It is said that Guang Dong women will treat their men better than any other woman."

"Sounds like a saying that Guang Dong women say about other Guang Dong women," I laughed.

*****

Xiao walked back with her drink and told Colin that Pei had wanted to lie down.

"Well, guess that's my sign!" he laughed, and stood. "We'll see you both later," and he strode down the beach.

I patted the towel, and Xiao sat down. We drank in silence, watching the golden orb of the sun start its descent into the ocean.

"I need to talk," she said so quietly I wasn't sure she had spoken..

"What?" I asked. "I'm ready to listen." I reached out for her hand, and this time, she didn't draw away.

"I have not been truthful with you." Her voice trembled, and a cold stone settled in my stomach. She stood and walked toward the surf. I rose and followed her.

"I don't know where to begin," she said.

"Well," I said. "The beginning is a good place."

She faced the setting sun, and began talking, more in a whisper. "My sister, Lily, you know, died." I nodded, and she continued. "She was killed by the Association."

Before I could say anything, she put her finger to my lips. "Please, let me continue, or I will not be able to go on." I took her hand, and squeezed it.

"She got involved with this man, and had a baby."

"Mei?" I asked.

I knew before I asked, and she went on. "Lily carried drugs over the border. A mule, I think. She knew our family needed the money, and she wanted money for Mei. This man didn't want a girl. He would have killed the baby, but Lily said she would do whatever he wanted. So, she began running drugs for the organization. We didn't know she was involved with these people, but we knew something was wrong. She wanted our mother to watch Mei. She would come and go. We didn't know what was happening with her."

Over the next half hour, Xiao told of how Lily decided she needed to get more money for the family and Mei, so during one transaction, she kept the money she was supposed to give to the clan leader. Instead of delivering it, she hid it to give to her family later, and told the leader that she had been robbed.

Tears welled up in Xiao's eyes. "Of course, he didn't believe her. He had her and Mei's father killed. He cut their throats."

"The clan leader? Of the Association?" I asked.

She shook her head. A chill ran down my spine. I had a feeling who the murderer was. But there was more. She had not told me everything. I grabbed her shoulders and turned her to me.

"What else?'

Now, tears were flowing down her cheeks.

"They said they would kill my family, even Mei, unless I worked off their debt," she cried. "That's why I was in the alley the night you and Trish were attacked. I wanted to protect you. I had been watching you and I knew you were a good person."

Something still wasn't adding up. Xiao had been protected, untouchable for a reason. Then, I knew.

"Clint? You and Clint?"

Now she was sobbing. "Yes, yes! But I never loved him like I love you. He protected me. And he likes you. There is nothing between him and me now. He knows I love you. I'm so sorry! I should have told you before, but I was afraid… I didn't want you to leave me!"

The cold stone in my stomach had grown. What was going on? Was there more to this? Who could I trust? I saw my plans for marriage and visas being swept out to sea with the surf, growing stronger in the twilight.

Xiao looked at me. Even with this gut-wrenching confession, she was not going to beg forgiveness. If I loved her, the ball was in my court, so to speak.

For the moment, it was going to stay in my court.

"So did you run drugs, like your sister?"

"No, Ben. I couldn't do that."

"Then how were you repaying her debt?"

"I would look out for police."

"You mean, you were a lookout, to make sure nobody interrupted gangland squabbles?" I asked.

"Yes. That is all. But I'm not doing it anymore. I am with you."

"But you were also sleeping with Clint."

"He was a boyfriend. I was not in love, though. Ben, I only love you."

"And the money—what did your sister do with the money?" I asked. That was the only thing I could process at the moment.

Xiao looked at her feet.

"Your family? They got the money?"

She nodded.

"How did the Association not know?" I could not believe that this was even possible.

More silence, then, again, the answer. "Clint?"

Another nod.

"And because of Clint, you don't have to work for them?"

I threw my hands up and started walking down the beach. Everything had changed. Visas. Marriage. Business. Destiny. Whatever it was that I was seeking, whatever it was that I thought I had found was not there, at least not now. Maybe later. Maybe not. I had to think.

I heard Xiao running up behind me. She took my hand, enveloping it in hers, matching my pace, not saying anything. I couldn't look at her. The coldness in my stomach had spread to my heart, freezing it, protecting it from harm. I had to sort this out, and I had to do it alone.

Nineteen

*B*ack at our apartment, far from Hainan and the truths that had been laid bare between us, I tried to get warm beneath the one sheet I had been allowed but it was futile. The couch was too short. My legs were too long. The room was too hot, too small, too cold. I could hear Xiao tossing and turning in the bedroom. Good. She deserved to sleep alone. Probably hadn't done that enough. She was lucky that even in my anger or whatever I was feeling, I allowed her the real bed. I should have kicked her out of the apartment altogether. Likely she'd find some other place to go anyway. Surely she could find another bed.

I was going to the U.S. to recharge. Revitalize. Reevaluate.

I tried to doze. The TV flickered and with heavy eyes, I watched a video clip showing Central Park, the oasis of green below our apartment. Police were standing around three bodies. A close-up of the men, their faces peaceful. Happy. Another video showed body bags loaded into a waiting ambulance.

My eyelids fluttered and I remembered a story I'd heard from locals.

Long ago, a prison had towered over Shenzhen's Central Park, beneath our apartment. The Box, as it was known, was a fat structure of cement and metal, crafted with the architectural grace requisite of dwindling communist largesse. Several hundred felons were imprisoned and sometimes tortured within its walls. Those unable to survive their sentences were buried without ritual in an enormous pit of lime and ancient skeletons behind the Box.

Murderers, rapists, and thieves were separated by only a few feet of concrete and steel from the mothers and children who savored the shield of jade trees and luxurious fescue in the park.

It was decided, eventually, that the prison was an anachronism, an eyesore representative of backward city planning, and further, the park, and the city at large, would benefit from its removal. Prisoners were scattered to other prison locations.

Emptied of its mortal contents, the Box was imploded and its original site became an ugly place. A bad place.

Rumor had it that ghosts roamed the premises, ghosts who were freed after the walls were taken down. To the dismay of city officials, everyone avoided the area. An invisible barrier seemed to surround the acreage, as if the structure still stood, in some invisible, phantom form. Even though trees were staked deep into the soil, and grass seed had taken root with large box hedge wound throughout, locals would not accept the park's new space. It was shunned.

Finally, I dreamed.

On this quiet, milky-moon night, three young men entered the annex. They had been dared to sleep on the grass above the former prison grave. It was an adventure. They were brazen, young, immortal.

The next morning, a woman, exercising her golden chow chow, had to let go of its red leash when the dog yelped and surged forward, hell bent in the direction of the old prison site. Finally catching up with her pet, she found herself standing near the young men's bodies. The woman abruptly stepped back and cried out. For only seconds, the dead had seemed alive. And if only for a few precious seconds, that awful place was also peaceful and beautiful and normal. The young men's faces, she said later, were grotesquely serene.

My cell phone buzzed. I jumped from the couch.

Confused, I couldn't say if the dream had unfolded in English or Mandarin, couldn't say if it had actually been a dream. A person has achieved a certain facility with a foreign language once they have dreamed in that language. So they say. I was not feeling very fluent in regard to anything, not in my business, not in my relationship with Xiao, not in anything, much less my fluency in Mandarin.

The phone! Still ringing. What the hell time was it? The light outside the window was dim but then, that was often true.

"Hello?"

"Did you see the news?" Napoleon's voice hissed in my ear. I recognized it at once. I tensed.

"No, why? What the hell...."

"There were three murders last night. You know the place. Everyone does because it's haunted. Many poor fools will think the spirits there did the awful deed. But you know better, don't you? And who else will die?

"Where are you? What are you doing, Napoleon?"

There was silence. I heard something brush past the apartment door.

"I want the money," he said. "You owe me money. Xiao is your responsibility, so her debt is yours. Or they will find your body in the park. Or maybe your lover's body," he yelled through our apartment door.

I was at the door in a flash and flung it open and as he stepped back in surprise, still with the phone to his ear, I gripped his neck with both my hands and slammed him against the wall, once, twice. The phone fell to the floor and before he could use his hands against me, I slammed him against the wall again, tipping his head back to take the brunt of the blow and once more—thud. I would wipe that anger off his face. Bang. And there it was, a flicker of fear in his eyes.

I twisted him around quickly and held both his arms behind his back and kept his face pushed to the wall. It was only because of my height and my anger and frustration that I was getting even this far. He was snarling and struggling but I held him fast, jerked his right arm higher.

"You are going to leave here, you cheap little shit. Your name is now on my list. You stay away from me and everyone I know. You think I'm a big dumb American? You think I'll run and hide and let you roll over anyone and everyone? You're nothing but a little punk. I've had enough!"

I threw him to the floor, then picked him up and scuttled him to the elevator where surprisingly, the doors opened. Several people were standing there and they quickly moved aside to make room for the dazed, bleeding man I shoved against the far elevator wall.

"He's going down," I said and pressed the button, then stood there a moment to be sure the doors closed.

I returned to the apartment, marched into the bedroom and started packing Xiao's things while she got out of bed, huffing and puffing around me, asking a thousand questions and getting not one answer and finally

I looked her in the eye and said, "I am sending you to your mother, to safety. Stay there. Don't ask me anything else." I knew Napoleon would return, and I didn't want Xiao in harm's way.

Then I grabbed enough things of my own to fill my backpack and after depositing a frantic Xiao in a taxi, I took another one to the airport to catch the next flight home to Missouri.

Twenty

*F*inally, I was in Missouri, in a real doctor's office. I wanted relief. I was all for Eastern medicine, but after I found out that the pills I got in the doctor's office in Shenzhen were for paranoid schizophrenics, I lost a bit of confidence.

"Would you like to sit down?" The nurse studied my face and read the pain. My head was pounding, my throat hurt, and I was seriously wondering if I was having a heart attack, my chest hurt so bad. My limbs felt like jelly. All in all, I was in bad shape.

After the examination, the doctor said, "It's the air, Ben. It's taking its toll on your body. I've not been in China, but I've read about it. The pollution, the crowds, it's completely different, and that's what I think the problem is."

148

"So what do I do?"

He gave me an inhaler for my asthma-type symptoms to combat the Shenzhen air, and a prescription for an antihistamine. He also advised me to use a neti pot for sore throats, congestion and ear problems, and chicken soup—the Midwest cure-all.

I thanked him and walked out of the office. I had prescriptions in my hand, and advice for Eastern-type remedies from a Western doctor. Who knew?

I stopped at the desk to pay.

"Do you live there, or were you just visiting?" the receptionist asked. Tightly—permed blonde hair framed her cheeks, emphasizing a fat, crimson mouth. She spoke quickly, her words projectiles flung from a sling of ruby lipstick.

"I live there part of the year." I leaned on the counter, afraid that I'd fall if I didn't.

"So, do you stay in a hotel?"

"Did. Now I have an apartment." I swallowed, and felt the bile rising, and breathed in quickly, easing my stomach.

"Oh. So do you have a girlfriend over there?"

"I do." Or so I thought. I also thought that this idle curiosity was getting out of hand.

"Has she been to America yet?"

"No, it's very difficult to get her out of the country."

"Are you sure you don't want to sit?"

"No. Thanks." I would like for you to hurry up, give me the bill and let me go home to bed.

"So why hasn't she come over yet, what's up with that?"

"It's the government. The U.S. government, not China. The U.S. embassy is very strict about immigration, especially those from China."

She cocked her head to one side, thinking about how best to sound like she knew what she was talking about. "I mean, they let people come and adopt babies left and right, so what's the big deal?"

"It's frustrating, that's for sure," Really, for sure, and getting more so by the second.

"The only way for us to be here, together, is to get married."

"Are you?"

"Am I what?" This was getting old.

"Are you going to marry her?"

"Well, she thinks she's getting to be an old maid, and she should marry soon, so maybe."

"How old is she?"

"Twenty-four." And this was her business because? I just wanted to leave, to go home to my bed, my parents, my mother who would nurture me and nurse my wounds.

"Well, you should marry her if you love her," the receptionist pronounced. I stifled a laugh. Ah, the joy of unsolicited advice.

I gave her a check, nodded, smiled and said, "I'm sure it will all work out."

My trip home came just in time. Not only was my body in need of reenergizing, but my soul as well. What was I doing? I had chosen China as my destiny. This was where I would seek my fortune. Then I met Xiao. My girl. I knew the relationship would be a challenge, but we were both working toward that, or so I thought. Now, it was all a lie.

Mom and Dad were happy to have me back, but they knew they didn't have all of me. Besides my physical ailments, which could be managed, there were the emotional ones and those weren't so easy. I could have shared our simple relationship, but when Xiao divulged her past, everything changed.

Now, it was up to me. I thought about Xiao there, waiting for my return, learning English, and hoping that someday she would be here with me. Ever since she confessed to me on the beach at Hainan, our relationship had changed. I did not want to condemn her. Everyone makes mistakes. All of her indiscretions had occurred before we met. So why should I judge her? I didn't know why. But I couldn't help it. And I couldn't talk about it. I ran home to Missouri under the pretense of health. I was here to heal physically and spiritually. I worried that underneath my need to renew my body and spirit, I was also frightened. I needed to face my fear.

*****

"My family thinks you're not coming back to China." Xaio's voice trembled with apprehension.

"Why do they think that?"

"I know you will come back, Ben." Now, a false bravado crept in.

"Of course I will." Would I?

"They say you have a wife in U.S. but I don't believe it."

"No, I don't have a wife."

"I know. When are you coming?"

"In about a month, OK?" Now I was committed. "I'll be leaving here in about thirty days."

"I miss you."

"I can't wait to get back to China," I lied. Missouri was familiar. Clean air. Honest. Safe.

We were still dancing around her big disclosure. I wasn't ready to deal with it. Knowing she was involved, or had been involved, with the Association made everything complicated. Was Al, my business partner, sucked up in this? I hadn't had a chance to talk to him about this before I left. I know I was sticking my head in the sand, but I just wasn't prepared to deal with all of the ramifications of Xiao's confession.

I knew why she was upset. Besides the obvious relationship glitch, the buzz of American culture was viewed through the faithless reality of television shows and movies. Americans were loud, they lived in mansions, shot guns, and cheated on their spouses. Everyone was rich, demanding, and got what they wanted. Why wouldn't she think I was resting poolside at my mansion, holding the hand of some white bride, and in the other hand a pistol, shooting into the open sky like some half-baked version of Scarface-meets-Dirty Harry? I could only imagine the gossip that percolated in her family's kitchen, and the awful half-truths steeped in the sound bites of televised Hollywood.

But, more than her family and her pre-conceived notions of America, I wanted to spend a couple of months breathing Missouri air, fishing at my parents' farm, being with my friends, barbecuing and doing all those normal, American diversions.

*****

I lost my cell phone. My computer died. The house Wi-fi router went out. Even my Volkswagen Beetle took a direct hit from the universe, when a freak windstorm dropped a tree on its hood. Maybe the universe was telling me something. I was reminded of a bit of childhood advice my mother had told me. "Be quick, but don't hurry," she would often tell me. "Organize your thoughts, make a plan, and take your time. When you rush, you make mistakes."

Phone, computer, and router were replaced. My connections to China now functional.

The car, however, I left parked. Long drives were replaced with longer walks and bicycle rides. I was weighing my decision to stay planted in Missouri or go back to China, and I wasn't going to make mistakes.

*****

I moved my fingers on the laptop's keyboard and clicked the Skype icon. The Internet connection had a slight time-delay, but the inconvenience was worth the free long-distance calls to Xiao. I heard her thin voice, light-years away.

"Hell-o?"

"Hey, how are you?"

"When are you coming?"

"Xiao, I'm going to stay two more weeks, maybe three."

"But you said you would come in thirty days. It's time."

"What do you mean?"

"I told you I was sorry," she said. "But you aren't here. My family says you won't come back. They say you have an American wife, and that you will forget me."

I could not keep the exasperation out of my voice. "Xiao, I don't care what your family thinks. What is going on here and what you told me in Hainan is much bigger than your family, and if you can't realize that, then we have real problems."

Silence on the other end. Finally.

"I'm sorry, Ben. I just love you so much, and I'm sorry. I keep telling you, but I don't feel like you hear me."

"I hear you, Xiao," I said. "Now you have to hear me. I need to be here. Your family is important to you. Mine is important to me. I can think here. I can sort things out. You have to give me some space. I do love you."

More silence. "I understand, Ben. Come home soon."

*****

Would I go back? My toy business there had great potential, or at least was on track. And I loved Xiao. I did before we went to Hainan. She confessed some things that were very difficult for her to share. Did I not trust her? Was that it? No, that wasn't it. It was male ego that was getting in the way. But knowing it and doing something about it were two different things. She loved me enough to tell me her story, and I backed off. Now, she's afraid she's going to lose me.

And, even if everything worked out, could she make it here in middle America? Could she survive the homesickness? The loss of her culture? How could I make this decision? How could I give her the best experience in the States? Would she adjust?

After a few days of rest, home cooking and my Mom's nurturing, my body finally rose from the ashes. I ran along the sun-speckled tree-lined roads around our home, soaking up the sun and letting the country air fill my lungs. With a new burst of enthusiasm, I dragged out the old clubs, headed for Forest Park and played golf. The next day, I dusted off the bicycle, clamped it onto the car carrier, headed back to Forest Park, and knocked out twelve miles, a feat that I could not have done a month ago. Feeling rather feisty, I celebrated my newfound health with a cold Budweiser at the Boat House.

Sitting on the deck overlooking the lake, I watched a speckled duck train its young to follow the line, follow Mother. The chicks orchestrated their movements like an instinctive water ballet. I worried over my instincts. Were they any good? Were my senses telling me to stay or go home? Do I want to go back to China? Is Xiao right for me? Do I love her? Yes, I do? Do I?

My cell buzzed in my pocket. I answered and heard the happy chuckle of my old college buddy, Andrew.

"Hey ya, Ben, how the hell are you? Feeling any better?"

"Yeah, man, I just got in some biking at the park."

"Why didn't you call me? I would have met up. I need to get off my fat ass and get some cycling in anyway," he laughed. "So, how are you feeling now? Did you see the doc?"

"Yep, and I feel fine. I didn't call you because I wasn't sure I'd even make it one mile, to be honest." And that was the absolute truth.

"Alright, hey, I'll see you at the usual place for dinner. We're still on for six o'clock, yeah?"

"Yeah. See you in an hour."

I closed my cell, went home and showered and changed, then drove to his favorite mid-town café, a tiny, twelve-table French restaurant. Andrew was there with a bottle of rhone, already open. He offered the man-hug thing, the weak, shoulder-patting exercise ingrained in our male culture. Instead, I pulled him in, and said, "Jeez, man, don't be such a homophobe."

"Hey, I'm not homophobic," Andrew replied, his cheeks flushed.

"Sure, you're not," I teased. "Anyway, man, how've you been?" We sat, and my old friend poured the wine. He swirled his glass and stuffed his nose in, breathed deeply, then exhaled with gusto.

"Good Cote Rotie, huh?" he asked.

"I think I haven't even tasted it yet."

"No one makes wine like the French. Any good wine in China? Do they even have wine?"

"Yeah," I answered. "You can get some decent wines at the European grocery stores. The Chinese wine is pretty bad, though. Might be good for cooking."

The dark wine trailed warmth down my throat and into my stomach, and I welcomed the relaxed feeling that followed. Roasted meat smells rolled across the room, and I realized how much I had missed this part of life. A good glass of wine. A quiet, elegant restaurant. A good friend. And real food! China seemed very far away now.

Andrew's voice brought me back to reality and we lapsed into conversation.

"So how's your girl," Andrew asked. "How's China? Business good?"

"Business is coming along," I answered. "I'm working on a solar train."

"A solar train, huh?" He sipped at the wine and frowned. "But a toy one, right?"

"Oh, yeah, I'm still working the toy angle. I'm just trying to close a multi-million dollar contract with a toy manufacturer here. You know, get the big sale, make my money, and retire."

"And your girl, Xiao, how is she?"

"Things could be better," I tried to figure out how much I wanted to tell him. He was one of my best friends, but still I didn't know how much I wanted to share with him. It was just too complicated.

"I want to bring her over, but the process is so damn hard. Getting a visa is ridiculous. The U.S. rules are bizarre. Their visa policies are so confusing. Ever since 9-11, it seems so random, who they allow to enter. But I think the process is worth it. I think, with some help, I'll be able to make it work."

"Have you found any Internet sites that could help?"

"I've done some research, but still, even with the best information, there doesn't seem to be any rhyme or reason to their rules." I examined my ice water, and chuckled. Ice. Clean tap water.

"Does she want to come over?"

"Things have gotten complicated," I said. "I don't want to go into them now, but things are not going well, and I don't know if they're going to go better."

Andrew just looked at me. I knew he wanted me to share any confidences, but he was a good enough friend to know that if I didn't feel right doing so, that was fine with him.

"I hear ya, man," he said, and we both raised our glasses.

The server poured more wine, and I devoured my salad; it seemed that all I craved were good, fresh vegetables and good red meat. I chewed a bite of butter lettuce and Roquefort cheese, the sharp tang of red wine vinaigrette fading on my tongue. We talked of friends we had in St. Louis, and friends who had passed by the wayside.

"Well, you'll like this one," I said, "A Chinese friend had a baby recently."

"Boy or girl?"

"Boy. They were really happy to have a boy."

"What, because they don't want girls over there?"

"No, I know many Chinese who have baby girls." I thought of Mei and her sweet smile, and wondered if she was in school, wearing her blue-and-white uniform.

"If it had been a girl, would they have kept it? All I hear is that the Chinese dump girls off, put them in trash cans, drop them off at the hospital. It's gender infanticide, the way I hear it. Do you think they really would have kept a girl?"

"I think so. The middle class is really growing over there, and more people are willing to keep their girls and pay the government tax to have more than one child," I felt duty-bound to correct this false assumption. "Anyway, they have this baby boy, and they asked me to give it an American name."

"Is that normal? Or was it because they knew you?"

"No, it's actually fairly typical. It's fashionable to have a Western name. But we had to wait thirty days to even see the kid."

"Why's that?"

"In Chinese culture, it's bad luck to see a baby before thirty days. So we waited. Guess what I named it."

"Ben?"

"Nope. I'm not that self-important. I gave the kid your name."

"You did?" At that revelation, Andrew set down his glass. "That's so cool. Now, there's some little kid in China who has my name. I like that. Maybe I'll get to meet him some day."

"You should." I said. "You should come over and visit."

Our first course was cleared. I waited for my steak to arrive. Good meat, common in America, was still a rarity in China. We clinked glasses, and we drank the wine, to my good health, of course.

*****

Even if things worked out, if I could get past the visual of her and Clint in bed, of her trying to pay off her sister's debt, if I could get past all that, would she want to come here? I had told her of the Chinese culture in St. Louis, but had I asked her what she wanted? Did I even know what she wanted, other than to be married?

After dinner, I drove back to Forest Park alone. I sat on Art Hill, a steep carpet of green, and watched picnicking couples share cheese and wine. A little girl ran by, pulling a red dragon-kite behind her. Cumulus clouds skidded into a rich, amber sunset, while a full moon began to pull up the purple night. The dragon gained altitude and underneath, a dog gave chase, playfully hurrying after the girl. The dog didn't care about the kite or the moon. He loved his girl. He had his priorities straight.

Xiao had changed my perspective on normal, everyday situations. She had a way of changing my mood by saying two words. She was consistent and loving and positive. Her feet were planted firmly in her strong beliefs about life and love and spirit, and my independent world, the egocentric, lonely, nomadic existence I had lived for so long was fundamentally and forever changed by her.

At that moment I realized I couldn't wait to get back home to China, to see her, to touch her. I realized that if I married Xiao, her family would come out of the proverbial woodwork. But so what. Marriage to an American would definitely create waves, and I hadn't met her extended family; Xiao had kept that part of herself hidden, a secret compartment of memory and family. Considering the family I had met—the earth-mother aunt, the ghost of her sister, could this really become any more bizarre? Marriage had always remained an abstract, something other people did.

Now, I knew I could do it. I knew I loved her.

Twenty-One

The plane roared down the runway and I took small pleasure in the half-empty seats to LA. I could sprawl without being rude and I had grabbed a blanket and pillow to jam behind my head.

Al had called, excited that our first order of trains had landed in U.S. stores. Our cash flow would be stabilized. I couldn't believe such a pedestrian concept could save a business and make the proverbial million but it was.

My mind and body were healed, strengthened by friendship, empowered by clean country air, and I was consumed by Xiao, the smell of her hair, the intimate touch of my lips to her neck. I wanted her now. As the plane lifted into the air, I felt the usual rush as though I myself were at the helm.

*****

After the boat trip and brief taxi ride, I stood on the sidewalk, looking up at the building, searching for which apartment was ours. Was Napoleon lurking in the shadows? I had contacted Clint and Al before I had even left the airport for the US telling them what had happened and warning them keep an eye out for the surly little bastard.

I wasn't afraid anymore, though. No, the only thing I feared was Xiao's rejection. I knew I should get to the office now to see how things were moving along, but that could wait. Al could handle things another day or at least, for another afternoon.

When I got to the apartment and reached for the knob, the door opened slowly. For a half second, I expected another encounter with Napoleon. I hesitated, slowly shifting my backpack to one shoulder, ready to swing it at the attacker.

She peered out at me from behind the door.

"Xiao." My voice came out in a hoarse whisper.

We both hesitated. Could we have the movie-style reunion of hugs and I'm-sorrys and then go straight to bed together? Would she sense the change inside me? My heart was different now, and wanted so badly to express my feelings.

No.

Leaving the door half open, she walked into the living room. I came in behind her, the door slamming on its quick-spring and I turned quickly to lock it. I dropped my backpack. She turned just in front of the window to stare back at me, then averted her eyes.

I went to her in frank admiration of her black miniskirt and stretch top and those killer heels she wore so easily. I lifted her chin, admired her hair, her long straight bangs, the punctuation of her eyebrows, her liquid almond eyes.

I wanted my mouth on her and my hands all over her. She waited, then backed away, and went to the couch. She sat down and picked up the TV remote. My heart sank.

I went to sit beside her, smelled the funk of the airplane on me but chose to ignore it and hoped she would too as I pulled her closer, my mouth at her ear, her cheek, zeroing in on her mouth. But she pulled away.

OK, round one, her point.

I went to the bedroom and showered and changed, then grabbed two cold Tsingtao bottles from the fridge, popped the metal seals, and sat down again next to her. Only the thin line between yin and yang was between us now. She remained rigid. Unblinking. Silent. And of course she refused the beer.

"Your hair is beautiful."

Silence.

"Your outfit is beautiful."

More silence.

"You are beautiful."

There was a flicker of something, not unpleasant, across her face.

"I missed you."

She pouted and stared ahead at the muted TV.

"I love you, Xiao. I have come home to you."

She pointed the remote at the TV, turned it off, turned to me and kissed me deeply, while her hands gripped the front of my shirt.

Twenty-Two

"There's a problem, Ben." Al was worried, his voice thin and distant. I was sitting in our office, having gone there for an update on the second production order, our Christmas payday. Now, that familiar cold-fist-in-the-stomach feeling was back.

"What's wrong?" I leaned forward, watching a smear of clouds scud across the sky. Below, hundreds of high-rise buildings blended into the murky sky. Rain was coming. I could smell it.

"It's the paint. Our rep in the States says the trains tested positive for lead."

"How is that even possible? This is the twenty-first century! Who uses lead paint anymore?" I jumped out of the chair and walked to the window, and tried to process the information.

"It seems our production line does. This isn't good."

"Really? It's not good? No shit! How did this happen? Do you know what this means? We're done! There's no way we're coming out of this without some major scrapes." I started pacing around the room to quell the nausea rising in my gut.

"There's going to be a recall, and after that, the finger pointing. We will take the heat for this, and it's going to do major damage to our business, our reputation."

I sat down again, leaned back on the sofa and stared at the ceiling. I looked at Al who was sitting at the desk, holding his head in his hands. He looked up at me.

"There's nothing to worry about, Ben. I've taken care of it," he said. He might as well be giving me directions to a restaurant.

"What?" I yelled again. "How can you say that?"

"Well, we do have something—the PR nightmare, but we can cover that. We don't have to worry about the money side. It won't be a factor."

I looked at him like he'd grown another head.

"Look," I walked up to him and grabbed his shoulders. "You can't tell me there won't be financial ramifications from this."

"Sure," he said, easing away from me. "But nothing permanent. Nothing that's going to sink the business. Trust me. I've already talked to some people and it will be fine. I've lived here for years, remember? I know who to go to."

"And these people would be?"

He turned, walked to the desk and looked out the window. "You don't want to know, Ben."

*****

It was late morning when I got back to the apartment. Xiao was asleep. She hadn't gotten home from her hostess job until 6 a.m., and would go back at 6 p.m. I hoped Billy's hammering wouldn't wake her.

Billy's hammering. Something was wrong. It was eleven in the morning, and it dawned on me. There was no hammering. I felt a cold chill spill down my spine. Shutting the door to the apartment, I locked it and ran upstairs.

I knocked on Billy's door. It was unlocked and I pushed it open.

"Billy. Are you there? Hey, Billy!" I stepped inside, and the familiar scent of fresh lumber hung in the air. Someone had trashed the room. The sofa was on its end. His stereo was smashed on the floor. Kitchen cabinets were open, with dishes and pots strewn about on the floor. My heart pounding, I entered his bedroom, and leaned against the door jam at what I saw. Dresser drawers were open, clothes spilled out, but worse, the mattress torn to shreds with the batting and stuffing all soaked in blood. Blood splatters stained the walls around the mattress.

I walked slowly over to the bed, and wedged between the mattress and the wall was Billy—or what was left of him.

Gagging, I ran out the door, and down the stairs to my apartment. I locked my door and with shaking fingers, called Al.

"Al, remember Billy? The guy who lives upstairs from me?" I said in a whisper, not wanting to wake Xiao. "The one who borrowed from the Association?"

"Yes," Al answered. "What's happened?"

"I just went up to his apartment. He's been killed, murdered. His apartment was torn apart. What do I do?" Then I remembered seeing Napoleon the day Billy moved in. Billy. The business. Clint and Xiao. Xiao's sister. What was happening?

Twenty-Three

*C*lick. Click. Click. There was the sound. Soft as a hush, but just loud enough, familiar enough to wake me. It was the invisible stilettos. Click. Click Click. They were crossing the floor in the living room, moving closer, closer, pausing at our bedroom door.

I opened my eyes and looked full into Xiao's face. She slept, her face sweet in repose, smooth and pale as though she had just powdered it to perfection. I closed my eyes, assured and turned on my other side. I could fall back to sleep.

The heels again.

Then silence.

I opened my eyes and her ghostly face was right there, thrust close to mine. I could feel its nothingness. I sat up, awake now.

"Go," I said. "Go now."

She shook her head no, her hair falling around her pale visage as she floated from my reach, toward the window. She was identical to Xiao. But not her eyes—those were black tunnels. Empty. Lonely.

"Please go. It's OK. There's nothing to tell me. I know everything."

"OK," I said, easing off the bed and walking slowly toward the casement window where she was, her image blowing and flexing in the breeze like a curtain. "Xiao has told me everything, about how you… died, and I'm sorry I really am, and she's told me about Mei who is your daughter, and about the debts and the shame. But it's all paid off now.

Your child is safe. It's OK. You can go."

She dipped her chin, shook her head. Her refusal renewed the chill in the room.

I looked away, out the window, beyond this spirit. Unfinished business, that's what tied ghosts to a certain place. Unfinished. What was holding her here? Think, man, think.

She hovered closer, too close.

And then it dawned on me.

"I love Xiao. I won't leave her. Not ever. And Mei, I love her, too. I'll take care of them. I'll take care of both of them."

Ghosts don't smile. They don't frown or pout. The face is just there, more a suggestion than anything. But I swore I saw her smile, a glimmer, a shadow and then Xiao's twin disappeared, silently, floating, no stilettos. Gone.

Xiao woke, rustling the blankets, and I jumped.

"You OK?" she said, squinting at me.

"Yes, Xiao. I'm OK. Make room in there for me."

Twenty-Four

$\mathscr{A}$ chattering flock of birds, mah jong tiles were mixed and remixed on the table. My eyes followed the action, looking for a fourth matching dot to make a "kong" and win the game. Down to my last 50 RMB, I glanced across the table. Xiao had known the mobster for some time, and reminded me that we could borrow some RMB from him, if we needed a cushion because of the lead paint fiasco. Borrowing from a gangster? Taking money from a criminal?

Clint had set up the meeting, a way to make peace between Al and me and Napoleon. I appreciated the fact that he had taken a liking to me, given his past relationship with Xiao. At the moment, I would take any advantage I could get. I knew Xiao loved me. I just wanted to live long enough to give all of us a happy life.

I figured he wanted this meeting to ease over the fact that I had taken Napoleon to the woodshed, and this was a way for Napoleon to save face. At the same time, I had the distinct feeling there was more to this than met the eye. Napoleon wanted something else, besides the money I owed him, and watching Al, I could see he had an acute case of nerves. Of course, knowing that Napoleon may have had something to do with Billy's demise probably wasn't helping his state of mind. But still, Al's normally cool composure was missing in action.

I hadn't said anything about Billy's murder to Xiao, and while I didn't want her to know about the company problems, she suspected something or else we wouldn't be here.

While Clint was the king pin, there was only so much he could do, and the rest was up to us. Al and Xiao stood on either side of me while I played, intent on showing my mah jong prowess to Napoleon.

With a flourish, I pulled a dot from the pile, and replaced it with a dragon, lined up my kong, and yelled "Mah jong!" The other players stared at me, obviously not wanting to share in my good fortune. Xiao pulled my arm, a reminder to contain my emotions. I was grinning for the victory, but more for the sovereignty of my winnings. Al shifted from foot to foot, cautiously optimistic.

Leaning in, Xiao said, "You know Clint is watching out for us."

"I know that," I said, trying to keep the jealousy out of my voice. "I don't have to like it."

She brushed her fingers over my hand, and whispered in my ear. "Ben, I love you. You."

I looked across the table and smiled. I am well-acquainted with Clint Eastwood, I thought, and there's no end to the surprises, is there? Regardless of whether he was retired or not, he still wielded a great deal of power, and I hoped it was enough to keep Napoleon at bay.

The live wall of marble tiles was broken, almost depleted, and I was rapidly trading in for a bit of luck from the pile. I won the game, and looked across the room at Napoleon. I held up the wad of bills and started toward him. I hoped this would quell his murderous tendencies. I had beaten him, and won Xiao's freedom, along with my own. But the money was insurance. He grabbed the cash, displayed his trademark snarl, then glanced toward Al who looked like he might bolt.

I saw Clint motion to his entourage and they left the room, leaving him and Napoleon staring at one another, a true Chinese pissing contest. At some point, without a word, they both turned and walked out of the room. Al looked at me and I shook my head. We would play this out to whatever end was in store.

Twenty-Five

I didn't know she was coming. But sometimes the cavalry comes riding in at the right time, even if you don't know you need them.

Such was Mom's arrival. She came out of the blue to touch down without any warning and called me from the airport to say she was in Hong Kong on her way to visit me. I could never have explained why but I felt some inexplicable sense of relief.

She was laughing on her cell saying she had no idea what to expect but that she was loving every minute of her trip and would find her way all the way to our apartment. Now Xiao and I stood in the park across the street from our building, waiting, waiting, one foot, then the other kind of waiting for her taxi to pull up. I didn't ask how; she had somehow managed to get the directions, explaining that she was indeed proud of managing her travel plans right down to the detail.

Xiao clutched my hand nervously, then unclenched her fingers long enough to dry them on her pant leg, then returned to her death-grip on my arm. I didn't mind.

Xiao kept saying that this was her chance to be a good ambassador for her country, and she stood there on the sidewalk, practicing a few English phrases over and over that she had mastered long ago: "How are you?" "Welcome to my country." "Welcome to my home." "Would you like a drink?" "I am so glad to meet you." "Here, let me help you with that." That last phrase made me laugh out loud. How often would Xiao be using that phrase?

"Relax, Xiao. Don't worry. Your English is fine. She will take one look at you and fall in love with you."

"Like you did, Ben." It wasn't a question. I was glad. I pulled her in, and kissed her forehead.

Mei was perched on my shoulders, holding still and being quiet, which was very unusual. The kid was normally a live wire from the moment she awoke until she was tucked into her bed at night.

Did the three of us look like a family? Did I fit in with the girls in my life? What would Mom see? She would tell me. She'd get me off into a corner and quiz me, size me up, ask one of her mom-special questions that would have me telling her stuff before I realized it. Yeah, there would be no holding back on what she thought. Or, she was going to go wordless on me, march into our room, pack me up and try to whisk me home to the U.S. Nah. Mom was smart.

Xiao was giggling with frustration but there it was, coming around the corner, flying down the street—Mom's taxi and I knew it was hers because her gloved hand was poked through the window, waving at us. She jumped out of the car the very second it stopped curbside and hurried toward us, grinning, and hugged me, her carry-on bag banging against me as she said my name over and over and Mei, still atop my shoulders, pulled my hair to keep her own balance.

"And who's this?" Mom said, looking up at Mei, and "Who's this?" she said, looking at Xiao and opening her arms. Xiao hesitated, then offered a slight bow. I would tell Mom later about the hugging thing in China.

Mei scrambled from my shoulders and stood looking up at this tall stranger, also very white, but oh so very smiley.

"Mom, this is Mei," I said, kneeling down to put my arm around the little girl.

"And this must be Xiao," Mom said, stepping back to look at Xiao and then at me and then at Xiao. This was going to be OK.

Xiao kept smiling, a rather fixed expression and mumbled, "Welcome to China."

"Thank you, Xiao," Mom said. "You have no idea how thrilled I am to be here. And don't worry, either of you. I have a room booked at Ben's favorite hotel not far from here so I won't need to take up space with all my stuff, and me!" She laughed.

The cab driver appeared at her elbow, having stacked her three huge bags on the sidewalk. I paid him, then began loading up for the short trek across the street and up to the apartment. The nervous smile twitched across Xiao's face like heat lightning.

"Mei, would you hold my hand and walk me across the street?" Mom asked, and Mei skipped with delight to hear her name and rallied immediately to do as she was asked. Xiao smiled broadly to see such immediate acceptance and before our little group set out, she went to my mother and embraced her. "Welcome to my country," she said. Mom was surprised and pleased. She is a quick study my Mom.

"When will we go to the hotel?" Mei asked.

"Ssssh, not now. First we treat Mother to a gorgeous home-cooked meal," Xiao explained. "She needs relaxation. Then we'll take her to the hotel. It will be a big adventure, OK?" Mei began to sing as we crossed the street.

"Very traditional song for queen mother to hear," Xiao said. Mom smiled at the reference to "queen" mother.

Mei was still singing in the elevator, and down the hall and into the apartment, where upon seeing the place, Mom clapped her hands and cried, "It's just as I pictured it." Well, I don't know what pictures Mom had been looking at and I had no idea what she expected, but I was glad for her approval.

Mei finished her song while jumping up and down on the couch as I stacked the bags by the apartment door. And then she jumped to the floor, ran to Mom and promptly threw up all over her. Xiao jumped. "Oh! Oh, no! I am so very sorry, so sorry, let me help clean up."

"No, no problem, here, I'll just use my scarf," Mom said, but Xiao ran to the kitchen for a towel. Mei sat on the floor and cried. I picked her up and held her. Having handed the damp towel to my Mom, Xiao next snatched Mei away and began wiping her face, crooning or scolding in Mandarin, I really couldn't tell which at this point, then marched Mei into the bathroom to clean her up. Mom was quiet and dabbed at her dress and I wondered if she was having second thoughts, about everything.

"She's a very beautiful little girl," Mom said as I joined her now on the couch.

"I know. But she's very nervous. She tried so hard to impress you, I think she just got a little stressed out."

"'Scuse me, Ben and Mother," Xiao said, leaning into the room. "I am going to put Mei in the bed for a few moments to settle. Then I'll be back to make a fabulous supper for you."

"That child looks so much like her striking mother, doesn't she?"

"Yes," I said, not bothering to explain everything about who was who. Not yet.

*****

Later, on the way to the hotel, it was just the two of us. Xiao had promised a visit to the queen mother tomorrow.

"I'm just saying, Ben. Are you prepared for this? A ready-made family? Do you love her? And I don't just mean Xiao—she's beautiful and wonderful—but she comes with baggage, Ben, she has a little girl. Can you do this? Are you sure?"

"I am."

"Alright, Ben," she said, tapping my knee. "Alright."

We were silent and comfortable together for the rest of the ride.

It was George himself who assisted with Mom's bags. She was full of pride that her son knew the hotel staff and I wondered briefly where Mr. Johnson was tonight. I wanted him to meet Mom.

George told my mother that her trip was very significant. Her presence, the company of the White Ghost's mother, was cause for celebration. He bowed. She grinned and couldn't stop smiling.

Later she whispered behind her hand to me, "What's the big fuss, Ben?"

"You're the big fuss. Enjoy it. This is a huge honor for them to have you. Mothers are particularly revered here. Besides, you are the gui-loa's mother."

Once in her room with her bags unpacked and everything stashed in tiny drawers, Mom declined a rest. She wanted to see the city. It was a warm summer night, she politely ignored the pollution, and though I felt at a loss for anything to show her, she was enraptured.

"Everything's so big, Ben. So big. I had no idea. It's beautiful here in its way, and there are so many people. It's just so wonderfully different, Ben." She held out her arms as though to embrace it all.

"Mom, welcome to China."

She turned and kissed my cheek.

"Son, what have you gotten yourself into?" she said, grabbing my arm as we walked together. "This is something. Some. Thing. Amazing. I don't know how you could take such a fantastic leap of faith, and just, well, relocate here. I would have been terrified, Ben, really."

"I was, Mom, I was terrified. I'm just now getting my bearings."

*****

As the train flew along, Mom put her hand on mine and looked out the window until suddenly, we were coming into Beijing. She asked about Tiananmen Square, and would we see it, and then, "What about the Great Wall?" I patted her hand, and told her in the local vernacular to "take a relax."

Xiao led us to the ghost market. Actually translated as "black market," she described how in the early morning hours, when the mist thickened the air, flashlight beams cut through the near opacity as deals were made in the small stalls. Among the traders were peasants who had looted the crypt of ruined buildings to trade the 100 B.C. trinkets and had brass sparrows, small pottery, and authentic charms. The government hadn't clamped down on them and a tidy sum was made on the Europeans and Americans who were thrilled to take home a treasure.

"Often," Xiao said, "foreigners leave with fakes." But what was the real trouble in that? Once the porcelain plate or golden sparrow had found its way onto a bookshelf in a city or small town in the U.S., it might as well be real.

Mom shook her head. She was enjoying a certain amount of disbelief and awe at the country that was slowly unmasking itself.

The market stalls were a maze. Many stall owners sub-leased the space and made as much money from the rent as they did from selling trinkets spread out on homemade quilts. Xiao pointed out the trustworthy vendors and explained that many of them hired friends to play the role of interested hagglers, just to draw attention to their wares.

Mom pointed to a nearby booth, and I followed her gaze to a row of tiny gold figurines tied with red ribbon and dangling from the stall's ceiling. There were animals of all sorts: horses, dogs, chickens, dragons, and birds that twisted and turned and held the light for seconds. I reached for a small gold dog, thinking fleetingly of my old dog. There were miniature Fo dogs, too. I knew about the Dogs of Fo, mythical creatures who were neither dog nor lion but resembled both. Typically appearing in pairs, they owned a cruel side but were revered for their strength and ability to endure and protect, particularly in terms of guarding an empire. I bought two Fo charms, in keeping with their duality—one for Mei, one for me. We wore our dog necklaces the rest of the day.

******

Later that night, after a four-hour, twelve-course meal, Mom and I reclined in our chairs while Xiao tended to Mei's bedtime story.

"Ben, I can see why you love China."

"Yeah." I didn't know what else to say. The night was soft, the sky was indigo, the city was silent. "Now I have a question for you, Mom."

"Mmmmm?"

"Why did you come to China? Why did you travel all this way?"

"To experience the beauty. To understand my number one son better," she said, smiling. "Because I didn't know how long you would be here, in this place."

"I do love it here," I said.

"And I can see why you love Xiao, I mean, I can see that you do love

Xiao."

I turned to look at her. "Should I marry her?"

We could hear Xiao singing in the next room, something low and slow and sweet.

"Only you can know that. If you want approval, that's another thing. But don't rush."

"I want to take them to America to see if they like it there."

"Does Xiao want to go?"

"She seems excited about it. But what if the only way to get her back home, to my home, is to get married? What if she hates St. Louis, gets homesick, and wants to come back here to China?"

"I don't know. I can't predict that." She shook her head and clicked her tongue. "But, nothing ventured, nothing gained."

"Huh? Oh." It was one of those things she said, like leap of faith, make a joyful noise, follow your heart the list of Mom's quotes went on and on. Suddenly, all her little sayings seemed appropriate, and thematic.

And I made my decision then and there. Without saying it aloud.

Mom was quiet in her chair, smiling.

Twenty-Six

"**Y**ou are lucky," the ticket-lady said. The train was delayed, and we boarded, our backpacks neatly organized for a short trip. Xiao touched my wrist and looked at her feet. "We are lucky," she said, "Great luck. Good year for that."

Our silver train, a decades-old diesel-electric, sat faded and worn on its rails. We strapped our packs to our chests, and huddled over them, blocking pickpockets. The smell of wet carpet, sweat, and muddy barnyard odors. Across the aisle, a man snipped at his fingers with nail clippers. Passengers coughed and hacked, the product of the ever-present polluted air. Surreptitious vendors hawked knockoff Prada purses, cheap imitation Rolex watches, snacks, and bottles of some homemade aperitif. Once security spotted them, they vanished.

An attendant shoved a drink cart down the aisle, but nobody bought anything. Passengers moved out of the way, some fell and sat on our laps for a moment, and I tried to breathe. Please be over soon, I thought.

We cracked our smeary window a bit, and relaxed, and waited for our stop.

*****

One-forty and we jogged to the embassy, raced up the escalators, and stripped down to our t-shirts and pants to shuttle through a security checkpoint.

Xiao cleared, but I didn't pass inspection. The officer glared and poked his finger at me. "Bomb. In bag."

"No bomb! Toy battery. From my factory."

A security detail probed my backpack, and carefully dissected the contents, like pre-med students probing through a cadaver for a cancerous organ. They found the offending thing and screened it for acetone, peroxide, and sulfuric acid. "Battery. Not bomb. You go."

Two o'clock, and a man was pressing the "closed" sign to his door-window. Xiao and I raced to him, and I yelled to the man that I was single and needed a sworn affidavit. He gave me an amused glance, paused, and opened the door. He walked us to a barred window, smiled, and whispered to the man behind the gated window.

"Have you ever been married before?"

"No, never been married."

He grinned, and I saw the decay of his incisors and thought about the Opium Wars and the generational curse of poor teeth. He stamped a red mark on my form and passed it through. Xiao smiled, completely unnerved and elated. We were headed to Yang Jiang. We needed her parents' blessing before we could complete our journey.

*****

We decided to ask her father and mother in the traditional way. I had five hours to stumble over the alien words, a Cantonese dialect with its individual verbal twists, country words. They would not understand my English or Mandarin. I thought of middle Missouri then, and cow towns, and Tastee-Freeze, and the secret language of small towns, the gossipy tongues wagged with the weight of collective knowledge and intimate nods.

Xiao squeezed my hand and reminded me of the traditions. She was the oldest sibling, and should be married before the next youngest sibling had a chance at matrimony. Yung was stuck—he couldn't marry his girlfriend until his older sister was betrothed. Also, she had said, this Chinese calendar was the Year of the Dog, the luckiest year to get married, and traditional Chinese follow traditional timing.

Fouling the air, two-stroke scooters buzzed alongside our lumbering bus, a beast bottlenecked in the morass of noise and humanity. I had avoided this for nine months, and many things had changed. Built over rotting trash piles, more buildings had replaced gardens of banana trees and tin roof shacks. Little startup factories stamped out metal parts. Rusted taxis poked from alleyways, and many people wore medical masks.

Humid air poured over the taxi's windshield, and the driver rapped his hand on the side of his door, and cheerily sang along with the radio. Did they all do that in this city? Tires rolled over treacherous streets crammed with all matters of transportation. Tin can cars of dust and motor oil and gasoline. Windows opened and cool, humid winter air flooded inside. I wiped sweat from my eyes, and wondered how I could be so damn warm on such a balmy day. Both hands clutched my pack, and I found my water bottle inside, took a big drink and offered some to Xiao, but she shook her head and gave me a weak smile. In this case, getting there was definitely not part of the fun.

Xiao's family smiled and waved as we pulled to a muddy road beside a windowless building. We climbed a flight of stairs into a small living room of concrete unpainted walls. Overseeing the sofa was an old Chairman Mao poster, the only thing that had the audacity to cling to the walls.

Her mother was across from us, in an ornate wooden chair, her father to the right, and sister and brother to our left, and the child, Mei, clung to my back.

"We have something to ask you," Xiao said, and turned to me. "Go ahead, Ben."

I looked at her parents and my throat was dry and I wanted the water bottle buried in my pack but I blurted out the question, in their local dialect:

"Wo ke yi he ni de nu er jie huan ma?"

Father turned to Mother, and his voice was loud and his brow creased. Mother smiled, like some '50s housewife, in black and white, one eyebrow a bit higher arched above the other, her eyes placid. And then everyone began talking at once. A cacophony of words, like the sound of wind and bamboo and rice paper ripping. I asked Xiao to please translate.

"My father did not understand what you meant at first. He thought you asked if you can marry him, and then mother said 'goofball' and that you mean to marry Xiao. Me, not him."

"Then what did he say?" I was anxious, and sweating.

"He said of course you can marry me!"

"What did your mother say?"

"She said that would make her most happiest mother in the world. Wouldn't have to worry about me." I slid back from the wooden couch and started to feel my hands again.

Her father poured hot green tea from his faded thermos. Local water, swirled into an undrinkable potion of boiled pollution blended with tea leaves. I smiled and took my cup and sipped loudly and spilled some on my shirt. At least I could look as though I was drinking the rancid stuff, I thought. The family began shooting local language at each other, but I could not understand anything. The sun was moving, and we had to find the courthouse, file the paperwork, and get our marriage license the next day. Before her parents could announce a dinner of fish eyeballs, I suggested the seafood restaurant on the corner.

*****

The government building was new, and smelled of fresh concrete. Hard wooden chairs guarded our destination, and as we waited on them, I wondered if every surface had to be so hard, so immovable. Comfort smacked the divide between poverty and middle class. The government, I figured, gave little thought to personal placation. A skinny man passed by, and Xiao asked when the office would reopen.

"Soon the lady will be here," he said.

One hour later, and the popping sound of hard heels echoed. A tiny woman, dressed in the government uniform of Drab moved toward us, a load of file folders wrapped in one arm, and the other free and moving with a soldier's rhythm. Xiao spoke first, in the local dialect. I

186

interrupted and asked if they would both speak in Mandarin, so I might understand.

Xiao handed our paperwork, and we followed her into the office and sat in a second set of twin hard chairs. The lady squinted at her computer screen, jabbed at the keys, and asked for our passports. Two minutes creaked into ten. Something was wrong, and she opened her desk and pulled out a goliath book. Blood-red cover. A million pages.

"The rules have changed, the paperwork's wrong," she said.

"But we followed the website's directions. What do you mean?" I demanded.

"Yes, but the law changed for foreigners."

I said, "How many foreigners have you married here?"

She said, "No Americans, Europeans mainly, but no Americans." She thumbed through the monolithic rulebook and her face began to squeeze tighter. Twenty minutes later, with an assistant over her shoulder, she was looking for the amended rule that said a gui-lao had to furnish a unique certificate, one signed with more authority than a simple U.S. Embassy official. Xiao began to smile a bit, and began to talk to the woman. Collective knowledge. Small town gossip. Sugar.

The lady yelled over to her assistant, "Did you find the rule?"

"I looked through the whole book and didn't find anything!" He yelled. The boy's desk was a sculpture of sloppy paper stacks and books and a newspaper that he found more interesting than a government policy manual. Obviously, he had no interest in helping. The lady sniffed at him, and began to attack her computer keyboard with vigor. She filled out a marriage application for the government, her terminal screen cursor careened over rectangles of Chinese characters. She finished Xiao's and started in on mine. "How do you spell your name?" she asked. My address wouldn't fit the form, but we eventually found a shorthand version that worked.

The lady sat back and smiled. She stamped our fingerprints in purple ink on a marriage book, and gave us a copy and a care package, a DVD with lessons about happy married couples and how to have good sex. We thanked her and her lazy assistant, and she said how happy she was that her hard work was done for the day, marrying the White Ghost and his Chinese bride.

We ran and grabbed a taxi. It was time to head back home to Shenzhen and plan our honeymoon.

Twenty-Seven

$\mathscr{A}$s we reached the door, she grabbed my hand and squeezed, then I pulled on her thick hair and brought my mouth to hers. I picked her up and carried her over the threshold and she laughed and playfully beat at me to put her down.

"What are you doing?" she demanded.

"It's an American tradition. I have to bring my wife over the threshold."

"What is a threshold?"

She kissed my cheek and, not waiting for an answer, asked, "Why? Why is it important you carry me?"

"I think it means I am showing my love for you by keeping you safe. Or maybe it's a macho guy thing. Or neither. I forgot."

"I like it. OK. You can carry me over the—"

"Threshold."

"OK, the threshold. And then I am going to take off our clothes and show you how macho I am."

"You don't get to be macho. That's for guys."

"I'm macho. Just wait, you'll see."

"I've seen your macho, and you're not so tough. I'm not afraid of you!"

She grabbed my hair and planted a big one on me. "Lucky year, Year of the Dog. You made me very happy."

"And now I get a lifetime to prove it, right, macho girl?"

Just then, my cell rang. Looking at the number, I saw it was Clint, and I knew our happiness was short-lived.

"Hey," I said.

"Get your things and be ready to leave," he said. "I'll be by in thirty minutes."

"Why?" I demanded. "Leave for where? We just got married!"

"There's no time now for explanations. Do as I say, and don't open the door to anyone," and the phone went dead.

I looked at Xiao. "It's Clint, isn't it?" she said. "We must do as he says," and she started pulling out suitcases.

"Wait," I grabbed her arm. "I thought I had time to pay your debt to Napoleon. I thought Clint would hold him off. It's only been a few days."

"Doesn't matter," she said, emptying drawers and throwing lacy underwear, colored blouses and short skirts into the open cases on the bed. "It's Napoleon. He has his own rules, and Clint can't control him. Never could."

Now she was in the bathroom, carrying bunches of bottles into the bedroom.

I paced the room, listening for my cell phone's familiar tone.

"Please, Ben," Xiao pleaded. "Do this!"

I joined her in packing, jamming my things into the suitcase and backpack. In a few minutes, my phone rang. It was Clint.

"I'm downstairs. Come quick."

We opened the door, looked both ways, then headed for the elevator. We punched the down button and waited, glancing down the hall both ways. The "down" elevator arrived a split second before the "up" stopped at the floor. We darted in, and as the door began to close, I saw Napoleon rushing toward us.

"Shit!" I yelled, punching the first floor button, praying th[e] would close before he could hit the "down" button. With[...] started, stopping at the several floors on its journey down[...] the door opened, we cowered in the back, trying to hide [...] running down the stairs to catch it.

After what seemed to be forever, the elevator st[...] floor and belched forth its contents of people who [...]nd lobby. Shoving and jostling, we ran out the front do[...] down the street.

"Here!" Clint shouted, a few cars away.

We ran for the car and just as we were ge[...] through the crowd onto the street. Pulling a [...]axi. us. His shot exploded into the windshield [...] caused mass hysteria with pedestrians pus[...] streets. quilt patterns up and down the sidewalks [...] the door locks and

We jumped into Clint's car, and [...] screamed at the driver to get moving.

"Just a minute," Clint said, and [...] his gun at Napoleon, who was sprin[...] his gun and looked at Clint. In th[...] go in slow motion, people runnin[...] from their guns as they pulled [...] and Napoleon dropped to the [...]

un[...] [...]eon burst and fired at [...]axi. The blast [...]attering in crazy streets. the door locks and [...]luced a pistol and pointed ward our car. Napoleon raised t second, everything seemed to rs skidding to a stop, and the fire triggers. Clint, however, fired first, und, his shot flying wide. I could see

191

Napoleon's face, his eyes empty, and a thick river of blood flowing from his forehead. His black and white caps split with, his destiny sealed.

Clint walked over, pulled something from Napoleon's pocket, and returned to the car. Sliding in to the front seat, he told the driver, "Let's get out of here."

Xiao grabbed him from behind and hugged him. I just sat there, [una]ble to speak, unable to comprehend what had just happened.

["I]'m sorry this had to happen, Ben," Clint was saying. "Napoleon [wa]s an assassin. He enjoys—or rather, enjoyed—his work a bit too [much. He]re are train tickets to Hong Kong for you, Xiao, and Mei. Also, [ticke]ts to Puerto Vallarta. Call it my wedding present." He handed [me an envelo]pe. My hands were shaking so hard, the paper slid from my [fingers. I] took it.

you

[I don't kno]w what to say," I said when I found my voice. "Thank

added. "I

can to help you get your family into the U.S.," he

"That's [tak]e awhile, so be patient."

ungrateful, but[...]us of you," I said. "And I don't mean to be

trying to make it r[...] Al? I know he made a mistake, but we were

Clint paused a m[...] don't want to leave him holding the bag."

inside coat pocket and [I] looked at Xiao. He then reached into his

said, "I took this off of Nap[...]ut a slip of paper. Handing it to me, he

the gift of life."   You might call it another wedding gift,

Unfolding the paper, I saw [...]eral names, all with lines drawn

through them. At the bottom, I sa[...] [m]ine. Above my name was Al's dissected with a line, and above that, Billy's. I was last on Napoleon's list, my name unscathed.

"He was coming to scratch your name off his list," Clint said. "And Xiao would just be collateral damage."

"But Trish, and their son Andrew—"

"Are fine, Ben. They are safe."

I swallowed, and imagined Al's lifeless body and the beautiful toddler and mother and I thought my heart wou

My heart ached for them, but I was glad to know t' wondered how I had been so lucky, how close I had

Napoleon's murderous quest. r the

"I'll have to call Trish as soon as we land. She business. That's what Al would have wanted." ery sorry

We all sat silent for a few minutes, then Cl ttle girl." about your friends. But you deserve to make a

Mei! I thought. Where was she? d up to the train

"How do we get Mei?" Xiao asked, :

station. d out of the car, we

"Not to worry," Clint said, and as sidewalk toward us, and heard... "Mal-Ma!" Mei was running d d threw my arms around she threw herself in Xiao's arms. I r both of them. t to get into the car.

Clint smiled, raised his hand a t me. "You take care, hear?"

"Hey!" I yelled. He looked t it sped away, disappearing in the

He nodded, got in the car it sped away, disappearing in the

congestion.

I turned Xiao's face to mine and kissed her. "Hi, Mrs. Stillwater."

She smiled and took from her red purse gold-wrapped candy and we gave them to everyone we saw as we waited for the train.

"Good luck," she told the world, "may the Year of the Dog bring much luck."

Epilogue

I held hands with both girls as we padded and squished across the warm Puerta Vallarta sand. We were somewhat shielded by the half roof of a small cave that ran close to the edge of the shore. We went up and down the sand all afternoon, kicking at the water, laughing, tasting salt, saving shells and we stood in the ocean up to our waists daring the waves to roll us over.

Later, as the sun set, we ate fish tacos and drank Bohemia beer. Mei smacked her lips over an icy lemonade.

I thought about the Grey Wolf and the coriander lamb dish that will always be one of my favorite meals in the world. But the Grey Wolf was thousands of miles away. Would we ever return to China, to Shenzhen? I didn't know, couldn't conceive of it at the moment.

I was giddy, I was slap happy, charged with a strange sense of freedom, like the day you graduate from college and the weeks before you have to find a job. Oh joyous limbo.

Our U.S. visa had been declined again, and our new paperwork was now at the bottom pile of thousands of applications. But I would never give up.

Here, along Punta de Mita, the northern beach unaffected by tourists, I was warm and there was nothing I'd rather have in my life than Xiao and Mei, my own yin and yang. In time, fate and hard work would get our small family to Missouri.

*****

My cell phone chirped, and Clint's voice came from somewhere deep in China.

"You will ride to Tijuana tomorrow."

Minutes later, as I slapped my phone shut and jammed it in my pocket, I considered how a sunset sky changed color so easily.

A border crossing. A chance to make a life together in the U.S.

Mei was shivering. I wrapped her in a beach towel, and the three of us settled on the still warm sand and watched threads of crimson clouds follow the sun into the horizon, dripping a trail of gold coins into the sea.

Author's Note

*T*he chapters in this book are all based on true events and my experiences in China over the past four years. My co-author, the master engineer of this novel, has embellished the stories and changed the names to make for a better story and protect the sensitive nature of some events.

During the first few months of my journey in China, my Western habits were turned upside-down. Daily activities such as eating, doing business, drinking, partying, dating, traveling, and living in small compact homes were quite a shock. Most importantly, I gained a new appreciation for the things we take for granted in the Western culture—the conveniences of fresh drinking water, access to a car, and all the food you can eat.

For the first two years there, my body and mind were shocked by the differences in the habits, pollution and the exponential growth of cities such as Shenzhen and the massive number of people living in one small square mile. I would leave a Chinese city for two months and then come back on a new super highway and find new hotels and businesses that had popped up after my short absence.

In China, I found fear, love, and ultimately, my destiny. As I write this, I await a response from the U.S. government concerning a visa for my wife and step-daughter.

- Gary Kellmann

Acknowledgments from Gary

This part of my life journey would not have been possible without first, my dear friend and co-author Michael Kuhn and his wife Nora who put up with my persistent personality and unusual writing style, journals, and stories.

A huge thank-you goes to a visionary, Mike Schrimmer, for encouraging me to step out of my box and comfortable way of life in the U.S. "Go pioneer China—it will change your life," he said.

My thanks to Dr. James Esther, for encouraging me to always "write it down" when I came back from China with stories to tell him and thanks to all in his office, especially Linda, who was so gracious to take care of me when I came back to the States with some kind of sickness.

Dan Lauer, thanks for that "kick" that I needed and being a beacon in this journey by encouraging me to make deadlines, or the book would never be completed. A big thank you goes to Andy Kolb for designing our website, Jason Holtgrewe for his finishing touches on the pre-press, Margaret Pundmann and Jill Loyet for your editing and support.

Of enormous support during this project was the Pals family. Anne, Harlan, and Kris thank you for providing me with a foundation that has allowed me to spread my wings and achieve my successes and your patience to help me through the tough times.

This book never would have happened without the inspirations and journeys with all my new friends in China who helped me when I was down and lost, especially at the Bossfield Hotel in Shenzhen and Liu Zhi Liang and Ye Chang Zhen who were my first and only friends when I came to China, and my new family in China who taught me the "Chinese way" even when I didn't want to learn!

And lastly, I thank my parents for giving me the building blocks for the passion and desire of what I do, and for teaching me the dedication and discipline and never give up attitude. I would have given up many years ago if it wasn't for you.

Acknowledgments from Michael

$\mathcal{F}$irst, I was forced to co-author this project; and I blame Gary and my wife, Nora, who insisted on my involvement, even after I declined Gary's initial invitation.

After years spent teaching my young students to use their imaginations and real-life adventures in stories, it was time, I realized, to fulfill a personal goal of authoring a "real" book. That, and the fact Gary wouldn't take no for an answer, sealed my fate for the spring, summer, fall, and winter of 2007, plus a few months into 2008.

For six months, I pored over Gary's elaborate travel journal, and together we crafted a work of fiction that stays true to his very real story. Hours were consumed typing into my laptop at Forest Park, in the quiet air-conditioned environs of the visitor center there. Brainstorming sessions at Pomme Restaurant in Clayton, Missouri gave way to hours-long writing marathons at Laumeier Sculpture Park, Forest Park, and my kitchen table.

Writing together, and by email, I began to research the enigma of China, relearning the legacy of its ancient civilization and modern metamorphosis from Mao's communist ideal to its current, legendary status as The Next Great Market.

As I write this, China is in the news for its forward-thinking Olympic facility designs, and also for its backward manufacturing oversights, including tainted toothpaste and toys coated in lead paint. It seems everything is touched by this enormous country. China is consuming resources at an ever-increasing rate, and its sheer size impacts all consumers and producers of the world.

Special thanks to Leigh Kolb for your efficient proofreading, editing skills, and encouragement throughout this long process. Thank you, Katherine Goedde, for creating our China map.

I could not have completed this novel without the encouragement and support of my wife, Nora.

Mom, Dad, thank you for instilling a love of literature during my formative years, for stocking our home with books and magazines, and for making the local public library a necessary part of my childhood.

About the Authors

Michael Kuhn, classroom teacher, entrepreneur, and writer, has conducted daily creative writing workshops for elementary students for over sixteen years.

Gary Kellmann, inventor of the world-famous Belly Lights and businessman who lives eight to nine months of the year in China. He sold his U.S.-based company in 2004 and then headed west to China. His inventions are sold around the world in retail stores and on TV. His latest inventions are focused on consumer and alternative energy products.

Find Asian-inspired jewelry from the White Ghost's journeys:
www.whiteghostinchina.com